f

Sophia Singh Sasson puts her childhood habit of daydreaming to good use by writing stories she wishes will give you hope and make you laugh, cry and possibly snort tea from your nose. She was born in Mumbai, India, has lived in Spain and Canada, and currently resides in Washington, DC. She loves to read, travel, bake, scuba dive, make candles and hear from readers. Visit her at SophiaSasson.com.

Also by Sophia Singh Sasson

Texas Cattleman's Club: Ranchers and Rivals

Boyfriend Lessons

Nights at the Mahal

Marriage by Arrangement
Running Away with the Bride
Last Chance Reunion
Making a Marriage Deal

State of the Union

The Senator's Daughter
Mending the Doctor's Heart

Discover more at millsandboon.co.uk.

Tempted by the Bollywood Star

SOPHIA SINGH SASSON

MILLS & BOON

First published in Great Britain 2023
by Mills & Boon, an imprint of HarperCollins*Publishers* Ltd,
1 London Bridge Street, London, SE1 9GF

www.harpercollins.co.uk

HarperCollins*Publishers*
Macken House, 39/40 Mayor Street Upper,
Dublin 1, D01 C9W8, Ireland

Large Print edition 2023

ISBN: 978-0-263-31341-3

11/23

FSC
www.fsc.org
MIX
Paper | Supporting responsible forestry
FSC™ C007454

This book is produced from independently certified FSC™ paper to ensure responsible forest management.
For more information visit: www.harpercollins.co.uk/green.

Printed and Bound in the UK using 100% Renewable Electricity at CPI Group (UK) Ltd, Croydon, CR0 4YY

This book is dedicated to all those
who feel that love will never happen
for them. It will. Keep your heart open.

Thank you to the awesome
Mills & Boon Desire Editorial team,
in particular Stephanie Doig.

It's lonely being an author but the
amazing community of South Asian
romance writers always keeps me going.

Last and most important,
I wouldn't be an author without the love
and support of my family.

One

"If you tell me there are more script changes from the Bollywood prima donna, I'm going to scream."

Gail dropped a bulging manila folder on Mia's pristine desk and sank into a chair. She was wearing her standard outfit of dark cargo pants, a black tank top and silver hoop earrings that were too large for her delicate face. Her jet-black hair was scraped into a ponytail.

"She couldn't even send them electronically?" Mia picked up the envelope, weighing its heft.

"Saira worked on them during the eighteen-hour flight from Mumbai. Using a laptop on the plane gives her a headache."

"How are you able to say that with a straight face?" Mia rolled her eyes at Gail and tore open the envelope. She fanned the pages, the sight of the familiar, perfectly formed, handwritten letters making her stomach flutter. *I had this tutor in India who made me practice my cursive for hours until I got it right.* It had been ten years since she and Saira had spent that month in Fiji. Ten years in which she'd finally moved on with her life. Mia almost hadn't taken this dream job because of Saira, but then she'd reminded herself that she had a reputation for being able to work with the angriest producers and the most narcissistic actors and actresses. Surely, she could handle Saira Sethi.

Mia threw the packet of papers on the desk, rattling the keyboard and mouse. "Shooting for *Life with Meera* begins in two days. The entire writers' room is ready to go on strike if I give them any more changes."

"We're not required to take her suggestions. Her contract gives her very limited powers, which she's grossly overstepping," Gail said carefully.

That's Saira. You give her an inch and she takes a mile.

"Want me to take the hit this round?"

Mia smiled gratefully at Gail. They'd met at the studio on the first day of their internship and compared notes on how many decaf soy lattes and no foam cappuccinos they'd fetched. In a city where relationships only lasted until the next job, they'd somehow managed to be friends for fifteen years. But even Gail didn't know about her history with Saira.

She stood and paced in her ten-by-ten office. The walls were covered with pictures and awards belonging to the previous director, Peter Denton. The carpet reeked of the cigarettes that he wasn't supposed to smoke inside. Mia stared at a picture of Peter holding an armful of Emmy awards. He held the record for the most Emmy nominations for outstanding producer and the most wins. In film school, Mia thought the key ingredient to success was talent, but she was wrong. It was opportunity. Shows succeeded when they had the budget to hire the best writers, stars and staff. Once a studio invested in producing the show, they spent money on marketing. Show popularity attracted better talent, and the cycle repeated. *Life with Meera* was Mia's opportunity.

Peter Denton had had to leave the show suddenly after his wife got sick. Mia had met Peter's wife at a party once; she was a kind woman and Mia sincerely hoped she recovered. But it was Peter's departure that had created this opportunity for Mia. The studio execs had finally noticed her and had given her a chance. It was her first big-budget show, and if the first ten episodes were a success, it would launch Mia's career.

Mia turned to face Gail. "I have to deal with Saira. When is she due in studio?" Mia had put it off as long as she could, but it was time to face her past, present and possibly her future. *Life with Meera* centered on a South Asian female lead, and the success of the show hinged on Saira's performance. She was the star. That gave Saira a lot of power, but Mia wasn't going to let Saira ruin her big chance.

"She's been here all morning—met with the studio execs, did the rounds."

Saira hadn't come to see Mia. At least she wasn't the only one avoiding their meeting.

Gail tapped on her phone. "Speak of the devil. She's in wardrobe, and Jessica says there's a problem."

Mia took a breath. Peter had let Saira run roughshod over him. They were already behind schedule and over budget because of all the changes she'd requested. It was time to show her former lover that the new boss wasn't going to tolerate her diva behavior.

"There's really no reason to call the producer." Saira's stomach flipped at the thought of seeing Mia. She'd been mentally preparing all day, but she wasn't ready yet.

The costume designer, Jasmine, was frantically tapping on her iPad.

"Listen, it's not a big deal. We can choose a neutral color like black." Saira began to unravel the fuchsia pink saree she'd been trying on but was intercepted by a wispy man with a pincushion in his mouth.

"I need to mark the hemlines," he muttered.

Jasmine shook her head. She was tall, broad shouldered with salt-and-pepper hair and lips that disappeared when she scrunched her face, as she was doing now. "Mia said no changes without her approval. The set designer planned around these wardrobe colors."

Saira stared at the full-length mirror. The costume room was much smaller than she was used to and felt claustrophobic, with racks of clothes and bolts of fabric cluttering the space. She had no idea what pincushion man was doing, marking hemlines on a saree. Didn't he know that she could just tuck the excess fabric and adjust it any way they needed?

"I'm not asking to change the whole saree, just the blouse." She pointed to the crop top, hating the sudden high pitch in her voice. She didn't want to sound difficult on her first day, but everything had to be right. A lot was riding on this project, her one shot at transferring her Mumbai stardom to LA. It had taken her five years to find the right show; she'd been patient, waited for the project that would give her the wide visibility she needed. But she'd made a mistake. Once she saw the final script, she realized that the network was making the same tired, clichéd show American networks had made countless times before. The script had the same stereotypical nonsense that previous shows proliferated, the kind of stuff that had ruined her sister's life. Saira wasn't going to let that happen. Even if it meant going to war with everyone on the show, including Mia.

The mere thought of Mia sent a jumble of emotions twisting and churning inside her chest. Could she handle working with Mia? Being in such close proximity to the one person who had once meant everything to her? They hadn't spoken in ten long years. Did Mia remember any of the passion that had consumed them both, or was Saira a distant memory for her?

It doesn't matter how Mia feels. Saira steeled herself. She couldn't afford to be distracted by thoughts of Mia. All of her focus and energy had to be on making the show a success. The past was just that, and she needed to bury it once and for all if she had any hope of unlocking the future she wanted. It didn't matter that her heart had been racing all day at the thought of seeing Mia. Saira had to keep things professional and not let her feelings for Mia affect the show. Could she hide her feelings from Mia? She lifted her chin in the mirror. Saira had been acting all her life. Her first memory from childhood was hiding under the couch from her parents. It hadn't been until a few years ago that she realized the memory was from one of her movies. Putting on an act for Mia shouldn't be too difficult.

Mia's image filled the mirror and Saira froze. Their eyes met in the reflection. Saira followed all of Mia's social media accounts using an alias. She'd seen pictures of Mia, had been prepared for the sight of her. Or at least she'd thought so.

"How is it possible that you haven't aged in all this time?" Saira turned, keeping her voice light. Mia was wearing skinny jeans and an untucked T-shirt with the name of the studio emblazoned across her chest. Her blondish brown hair was loosely tied into a messy bun. She'd never worn much makeup, but Saira didn't miss the fresh touch of pale pink gloss on her lips and the swipe of brown mascara that brought out the green tones of her hazel eyes.

Mia turned to the costume designer. "Jessica, are you finished with Saira?"

Saira's back was turned to Jessica but she was pretty sure that the woman was making faces. There was a slight twitch in the very corner of Mia's lips; she was trying to keep a straight face. Saira could almost feel the softness of that corner beneath her own lips.

"We need to discuss Saira's request on this outfit. It's for the first day of shooting, I don't have time to make these changes." Jessica stepped toward Mia, iPad in hand, her fingers dancing on the screen.

Mia cut her eyes to Saira. "What's the problem with the saree?"

Mia's tone was cold and all business. Saira's heart shrank. What did she expect after all this time? For Mia to throw everyone out of the room, embrace her and tell her how much she missed her? This wasn't a scene out of some romantic movie, and they weren't exactly long-lost lovers reuniting.

She took a steadying breath. "The blouse is the same fabric as the saree. It's too matchy-matchy. My character, Meera, is a stylish, young, Indian woman. No one like that would be caught dead in this old-fashioned style. You can replace it with a plain black blouse that won't take much time to make." If her tailor from India was here, he could do it in less than an hour.

Mia's mouth set into a straight line. "It's a fair point, but Jessica is on a tight schedule. We need to let it go for this episode, but she can go over the rest of the costume designs with you and we'll try to incorporate your suggestions in any of the outfits that haven't been completed yet." Without waiting for a response, Mia turned toward Jessica, issuing her directions.

Just like that, Saira had been dismissed. She gathered the silky material of the saree into her fists. *Deep breaths.* Arguing with Mia in front of her staff would just make her more confrontational. She needed to get Mia alone.

As Mia huddled with Jessica, pincushion man turned toward her. "Could you take this off now? I need to finish ironing it before I go for the day."

She gave him a tight smile. *This sure isn't Mumbai.* She was used to an army of assistants itching to please her. If anything, she longed for an empty dressing room, a break from the enthusiastic smiles and eager offers of assistance. One of the first things Mia had done as producer was cut her budget to bring staff from India. Saira hadn't argued because she wanted a break from the constant army that hovered over her. But now, as she watched pincushion man try to unwrap the five yards of saree fabric, she regretted her decision.

Saira was used to being scantily dressed in front of people. It was a necessity on set, but she suddenly felt conscious of Mia in the room. After taking off the petticoat, the long skirt worn underneath a saree, and the crop top blouse, she was left in a lacy black bra and matching panties. Pincushion man yelled for a robe. Feeling awkward, she pretended to study her forehead. Her agent had been encouraging her to get Botox before the wrinkles deepened but Saira had resisted. She'd seen too many of her fellow actresses get seduced by the promise of procedures and injections only to end up looking like puffed-up versions of their former selves. Five more years, that's all she needed her body and skin to give her; less if those years were in Hollywood and she earned in US dollars. Then she could finally be free to live the life she wanted.

She caught Mia's eyes in the mirror and held her gaze. Her pulse kicked at the unmistakable appreciation that was written all over Mia's face. Black lace used to be Mia's favorite. Mia walked to one of the racks, grabbed a blue silk robe and threw it at Saira.

Saira shrugged on the robe, watching with satisfaction as Mia's eyes darkened before she looked away. Turning around slowly, Saira smiled. "Is this a good time for us to talk? In private?" She looked pointedly at Jessica. Pincushion man was already walking out, nearly tripping over the trailing length of saree he hadn't managed to fold.

Mia shook her head, but Jessica was already making her way to the door with ill-disguised relief.

"Please close the door," Saira yelled, her eyes never leaving Mia.

She stepped toward Mia. "Listen, while we are alone, I want to clear the air." She swallowed. "About us…"

Mia stepped back, her eyes flashing. "There is nothing to clear. What happened between us was a long time ago. I've moved on with my life, and I know you have too."

Moved on? Saira had scoured Mia's social media accounts. There were plenty of pictures with friends, but none that looked like a girlfriend.

"I tried to call, email, text, even tried to reach you on social media after Fiji."

"You made your feelings very clear when you said goodbye."

Mia turned away, clearly bolting for the door. Saira's chest tightened. She was used to a laughing, carefree Mia, who could warm her heart just by looking at her. Had ten years changed her so much, or was it that Mia hated Saira? "I want to explain what happened that day in Fiji…"

Mia whirled, facing Saira. Her eyes blazed an emerald green. "You don't need to explain. Either you were lying to me when we were together, or you were lying when you broke up with me. The distinction doesn't matter to me."

The ice in Mia's voice made Saira go cold. They had to make peace, the tension between them wasn't good for the show. Saira had to make it right.

"It does matter." She stepped close to Mia and placed a hand on her arm. The warmth of Mia's soft skin, the shine in her eyes made Saira's heart flutter uncontrollably. She'd waited ten years to say these words. "I hate the way I left things between us in Fiji. The things I said..."

Mia moved Saira's hand away with such gentleness that her chest tightened.

"I don't care about the past. There's only one thing that matters, and that's making this show a success. Other than that, we don't have anything to discuss."

The words stung. But what really hurt was the pity in Mia's voice. Saira hadn't really expected Mia to welcome her with open arms. She'd been ready for anger, even hatred—but not the look of sympathy that was in Mia's eyes.

Saira stepped back, her throat so tight she wasn't sure she'd be able to speak. "I am sorry, Mia," she managed to choke out.

Mia took a deep breath. "If you're sorry, then forget what happened ten years ago and work with me on making this show a success." Mia gave her a steely look. "I received the script edits that you sent. I know there's some leeway in your contract to provide input, but the read-through is tomorrow and shooting starts the day after. It's simply too late to…"

Saira interrupted her, her voice cracking with emotion. "Mia, please, this show is important to me and—"

Mia cut her off, her tone icy. "Great. Then stop sabotaging it. Every time you want to change something, the script, the costume, the set, it costs us time and money."

Saira crossed her arms. She didn't know what was harder to take, the accusation that she was somehow purposely making things difficult, or the fact that Mia believed Saira would behave this way. Mia might be angry with her, but surely she had reviewed Saira's changes and could see what she was trying to accomplish.

"Have you looked at the changes I'm requesting? I've studied every South Asian show Hollywood has produced and they're mediocre at best. This show has to be different, and the way we do that is to..."

"Oh, of course you know better than all of us what's best for the show."

Saira's nails dug into her clenched fists as she struggled to keep her emotions in check. She could handle anger, even pain; what she couldn't quite reconcile was that the once warm and supportive woman she knew was now acting like every other know-it-all producer she'd ever worked with.

"I've been in the film industry for thirty years. I've done nine TV shows, thirty-seven movies, and I don't know how many guest appearances. Show me someone on your team who has more experience than I do."

"No one disputes that you're a great actress. That's why you're here. But acting is not the same as...."

Saira put her hand, palm out, toward Mia. If Mia was going to treat her like any other actress, then Saira was going to treat her like just another producer. "There's no reason to debate here. I believe my contract allows for final approval on all dialogue and mannerisms that relate to Indian culture."

Mia crossed her arms. "It's too late to make the changes."

"Then I suggest you consult your lawyer. I don't believe the contract specifies a timeline. You know as well as I do that scripts, costumes, sets…everything can be changed." She gave Mia a thin-lipped smile. Her bitch smile. If Mia wanted their relationship to be professional, then that's what she would get.

Mia narrowed her eyes "You're right. Everything can be changed. Including the heroine." She turned and opened the door. Just as she stepped out, Mia turned. "By the way, your husband called. He said he'll be here to support you on the first day of shooting."

Two

Mia slammed her door and stood against it, breathing deeply. Her heart thundered in her chest and she wiped her damp hands on her pants. Damn Saira! Mia thought she'd been prepared to see her, to deal with her, to stand up to her, but one look at that woman and Mia's stomach had turned to Jell-O. All she'd been able to think about was the feel of Saira's silky skin against hers, the way her mouth felt on her lips, the warmth of her breath on her core.

She slid to the floor, hugged her knees to her chest and buried her face in her arms.

What is wrong with me? It's not as if Mia had been alone all this time. She'd been with several partners. Beautiful women, available women, women who were comfortable being openly lesbian. She had no problem meeting people. The TV and film industry was a constant churn of writers, artists, interns, set workers and on and on. There wasn't a day that went by where she didn't have the opportunity to ask someone out, or get asked out. There was no reason to want Saira.

Twelve weeks. She just had to get through the filming. Peter would be back before the next season, and if the show was a success, Mia could have her pick of producer jobs. She'd make sure she never had to work with Saira again.

A sudden knock on the door made her jump up. Before she could even take a step, the knob turned and the door began to open. Mia quickly sidestepped to avoid being hit.

"What is it?" she snapped, still a bit rattled by the unexpected interruption.

"Sorry!" Gail stuck her head around the door. "You're supposed to be meeting with

Chris to go over the budget. You can't be late—you only have fifteen minutes with him."

Mia looked at her wristwatch and cursed. She hurried to the desk and picked up her laptop. Chris was an insufferable network executive who controlled the purse strings on the TV series. He kept sending Mia red envelope emails regarding show expenses, then ignored her reply questions. It had taken Gail begging, coercing, then finally bribing his assistant to get this meeting.

Mia nearly ran to the elevators, stabbing the buttons in frustration. There were eight elevators in the bank, and the electronic dashboard showed that none of them was close to her floor. Chris's office was thirty stories up. Even if Mia raced up, she'd never get there in time. At last a door dinged open and she exited onto the sixty-sixth floor. Mia had never been to this floor before, but she wasn't surprised to see that, unlike the commercial white square tile and gray carpet on her floor, the executive floor had hardwood floors with marble inlays, modern area rugs and polished leather couches and chairs in the waiting areas. The receptionist checked her ID and then pointedly looked at her watch. “You’re two minutes late. You will have twelve minutes with him.”

“Thirteen.” Mia said through gritted teeth.

“It’ll take you a minute to get to his office.”

Mia tightened her grip on the laptop. “Can you let me in so I don’t lose any more time?”

The receptionist took her time buzzing Mia into the inner chamber, which was separated from the outer waiting room by a glass wall. Another assistant greeted her with thin lips and pointed her to a slightly ajar door.

Mia hurried to the door, then froze. She’d recognize Saira’s fake laugh anywhere. The first time Mia had heard it was when a fan had recognized Saira in Fiji. Saira had pretended that she was *oh so happy* that the fan wanted an autograph and not at all concerned when she asked to take a selfie with Saira and Mia. *This is my childhood friend. She’s just like a sister to me.* That was the first time alarm bells had gone off in Mia’s head. *And those alarm bells are still clanking.*

“You must be Mia.”

Chris O'Toole was the stereotypical network executive. Average height, expensive suit that couldn't hide the middle-age bulge in his waistline, male pattern baldness that he clearly thought he had covered with a state of the art hair plug transplant. His voice was slightly nasal and immediately grated on Mia.

She stuck out her hand and mustered a friendly smile. "It's nice to finally meet you in person."

"Do you need a few more minutes before our budget meeting?" Mia looked pointedly at Saira and immediately wished she hadn't. Saira had changed out of the robe that she'd seen her in less than an hour ago. She was wearing a silky pearl white blouse with several top buttons open. Mia could practically see the drool from Chris's chin in the tantalizing dip of her cleavage.

Chris waved his hand dismissively. "The budget crisis is solved." He gestured for Mia to sit on the couch across from Saira. Chris's office was a spacious and stylishly designed room, big enough to fit most of Mia's apartment without much trouble. An L-shaped desk dominated one corner, with two sleek white monitors sitting atop it. The wall opposite the desk was made entirely of floor-to-ceiling windows, offering a breathtaking view of the distant mountain landscape. In another area of the room, a large conference table was surrounded by leather chairs that were far more comfortable than Mia's own desk chair. Currently, they were all seated in the living room portion of the office, a carafe of coffee and mugs bearing the network logo resting on the table between them. The air was filled with the invigorating scent of coffee and the warm aroma of whiskey.

"Saira has saved the day."

What has she done now?

Mia didn't dare look at Saira. She knew her gaze would wander down her blouse and she needed to keep her focus on the meeting. Instead, she locked eyes with Chris and asked, "What did I miss?" Her tone was friendly and composed, but inside, she seethed. How dare Saira go behind her back?

"Saira has agreed to reduce her fee by 32 percent."

Yeah, right. How many arms and legs did she ask for in return?

"That's quite generous." She looked at Saira, who gave her one of her dazzling fake smiles. It was the one she gave the cameras, the adoring fans—a toothy grin that left people basking in her glow.

"I'm just as invested in the success of this show as the network is," Saira said, setting the coffee mug on the table. "This way, there is room in the budget to make the changes that'll make the show better."

And there it is.

"Exactly what changes are we talking?" Mia shot Chris a look but his gaze was plastered on Saira. Or more accurately, the curve of Saira's breast that peeked through the V opening of her blouse every time she moved.

"Little things here and there." Saira's voice was sugar sweet. She met Mia's gaze. "Like the color of the saree blouse and the dialogue changes I requested."

"All those little things add up to personnel time and production delays." Mia couldn't keep the irritation out of her voice.

Saira narrowed her eyes. "Those little things can make the difference between the show trending in the top ten in online streaming or barely hitting six figures in viewership."

"Right you are," Chris said. "It is the little things that determine whether a show is good, or if it's great."

Mia bit the inside of her cheek to keep from reminding Chris that he was a financial weenie who probably couldn't tell the difference between a producer and a director.

"Well, thank you, Saira. I'm sure you have a lot still to do, so we won't keep you here any longer."

Chris shook his head. "Oh, no rush, I can cancel my next meeting, and I don't think there's anything more I need to discuss with Mia that we can't take care of over email."

Mia clenched her jaw to keep from saying something she'd regret.

Saira stood. "Actually, I am still a little jet-lagged. I should get some rest before the big read-through tomorrow. I'll let you get on with your meeting." She shot Mia a smile, one of her genuine ones. *Is it my imagination or is there an apology in her eyes?*

Chris made a show of walking Saira to the door. When he leaned in for a hug or a kiss, Mia wasn't sure which, Saira deftly sidestepped and held out her hand for a shake. Not to be deterred, Chris took her hand and kissed it, holding it to his lips longer than comfortable for anyone. Mia nearly laughed when Saira wiped her hand on her skintight jeans.

Chris walked to his desk, completely ignoring Mia. Not to be discouraged, she took a seat in the guest chair and placed her laptop loudly on the desk. As Chris swiveled in his chair, tapping on his keyboard to wake up his computer, he asked in a distracted tone, "Do we have anything else to talk about?"

Mia took a deep breath before responding, "Are you changing Saira's contract?"

Chris nodded, a determined look on his face. "Of course. I want to lock down her fee reduction before she changes her mind."

Mia pressed further. “Did she request any other changes?”

“Just some minor wording changes,” Chris replied nonchalantly.

Mia sighed. “Her changes are not that minor. We can’t give her more control over the show.”

Chris turned toward her, his expression hardening. “The show is already 21 percent over budget, and we both know unexpected expenses will come up during filming. Whatever Saira needs, find a way to make it work.”

Mia opened her mouth to lay out all the ways in which Saira’s salary discount would end up costing them in the long run, but the door opened and his assistant walked in.

“Good work, Mia, keep it up,” Chris said dismissively.

“Can I at least review the contract changes?”

“Ms. Strome, you’re already five minutes over your meeting time and his next meeting is waiting,” the assistant said, her tone brusque. Mia felt a hand on her arm, but she shrugged it off and walked out. She didn’t see the point in causing a scene. As a producer with little clout and even less experience handling people like Chris, she had to pick her battles. What she needed was to get a handle on Saira—that was a problem she knew how to solve.

She was looking up Saira's cell number on the call sheet to see if it was the same number she had stored in her phone—the number she hadn't quite brought herself to delete—but she needn't have bothered. Saira was in the waiting room chatting with Jason Brossart, one of the senior vice presidents. *Dammit.* That was the guy in charge of entertainment content. *What is Saira up to now?*

She stepped up to them.

"Speak of the devil," Saira said as Mia approached, and she braced herself. Had Saira complained to Jason? Unlike Chris, Jason had the power to remove her as producer. *Hell, he has the power to cancel the show and send us all home.*

Jason turned and put out his hand. "I don't think we've actually met, Mia. Saira was just telling me how wonderful you are to work with. Thank you for pinch-hitting for

Peter." Mia shook his hand and she found herself liking him. His grip was firm but not hard. Unlike Chris, who exuded a smarmy quality, Jason had warmth.

"It was a pleasure meeting you both. I wish I could stay and chat, but I'm late for a meeting."

As he walked away, Mia turned to Saira. "Thanks for putting in a good word." She meant it. Jason had the power to make her career, and even if Saira considered it a throwaway comment, he'd remember her name when it came across his desk in the future.

Saira gave her a small smile. "Whatever differences we have regarding the show, I want the very best for you, and if I can do anything to make it happen, I will."

Mia's breath caught. Saira's eyes shone and a lump formed in Mia's throat. This was the side of Saira that Mia had fallen in love with—the Saira who instinctively understood her wants and needs, who took genuine pleasure in doing something for someone else. It was easy to forget that Saira was like a kaleidoscope with constantly changing facets and reflections, depending on which way Mia was looking. The overwhelming, disconcerting feeling of being in Saira's orbit came rushing back to her.

"I was wondering…"

"Do you think we could…"

They both spoke at once, but Saira gestured for Mia to continue. "We should talk," Mia said.

Saira nodded. "How about dinner tonight?"

Mia agreed. "That sounds great. Do you want to go to the hotel and freshen up first?"

Saira glanced at her wristwatch. "If I go back to my room, I'll flop onto the bed and fall asleep for the rest of the night. How about we order room service and catch up over dinner?"

Mia's cheeks flushed as the image of room service dinners in Fiji flooded her mind. At the time, Mia had thought all the room service orders were because they couldn't stop having sex long enough to go out. She later realized Saira didn't want to be seen in public with her. Still, the memory of those dinners had tormented her for years. Especially the way they had chosen to eat dessert.

Tempting, oh so tempting.

Three

Despite it only being five o clock, the Thai restaurant was full, and they ended up at a bar table, which was noisy and packed with people. Not a great ambience for a heart-to-heart but it would have to do. If this were Mumbai, Saira would've gotten the best table in the house. *There will come a time when a crowd of fans will greet me in LA too. As long as I keep my focus on this show.*

Saira had thought she was ready to face Mia, but the day had been far more excruciating than she'd anticipated. The last few hours had been a roller coaster of emotions, memories and regrets flooding her mind with a dizzying intensity. The anger in Mia's eyes was palpable, and it cut through Saira's heart like a knife. It was clear that Mia was so focused on maintaining a wall between them that she wasn't being reasonable about the script and costume changes. Saira had to make it right; she couldn't let the weight of her past mistakes ruin her future. She had to make Mia understand why she'd left the way she had.

They ordered drinks—a Diet Coke for Mia and a mojito for Saira. Mia was staring at the menu as if it was a legal contract she was about to sign.

"Don't even pretend you're not getting the pad-see-ew."

Mia looked up at her defiantly. "Actually, I was thinking of the shrimp pad thai."

"Since when do you eat seafood?"

"A lot of things have changed in the last ten years, including my tastes."

You haven't changed in the slightest bit. You just want me to think you have. "So tell me what's new with you. What have you been up to since we last saw each other."

Mia took a long sip from her supersized

Diet Coke, the sound of the straw sucking up ice and soda amplifying the silent tension between them. "Ten years is a long time. There have been a lot of milestones in my life:—my first show as producer, one Emmy nomination for assistant producer…many, many, girlfriends."

Saira bit her tongue to keep from asking exactly how many.

"Anyone serious?"

"You know how it is, Saira—it's so easy to think you're in love in the moment but it's really not much more than relationship excitement."

Her chest tightened as Mia flung her own words back at her. Words she had carelessly chucked at Mia in Fiji. They were the words of a young woman who hadn't yet understood what love was.

"I didn't mean what I said back then," she said quietly.

"You meant it when you said it."

Saira shifted under Mia's unrelenting stare. *She's still so angry at me. How do I make her understand?*

"I was scared and confused. You were my

first girlfriend…my parents didn't know I'm a lesbian. *I* didn't fully understand my sexuality…."

"And you're just as confused now as you were back then. You're married to a man, for goodness' sake. You married him, what, two days after you broke up with me?"

"It's not a real marriage!" As she caught a few people turning around to look at her, Saira lowered her voice. "Rahul and I are good friends. He did me a favor—after the pictures of you and me in Fiji, there was an uproar in India. There were death threats against me, against my family. People aren't very tolerant in India, and it was even worse ten years ago. *Six months* after I returned from Fiji, I needed to do something drastic to save my career, to protect my family. Marrying Rahul was the only way to calm the public outcry against me."

"Do you think it was easy for me to come out as a teenager? Do you think things weren't difficult here? I know it's not quite the same, but there is plenty of stigma and hate crimes here as well. I'm not saying it's easy, but it is a choice—no one is forcing you to live a lie."

Mia would never understand. She'd grown up in America, where the streets were safe and girls whose parents disowned them had choices other than prostitution or begging. If Mia was the one getting death threats, the police would protect her, not help the perpetrators. She would never understand what it was like to be in Saira's shoes. To live in a country where she could go from being a loved icon to a symbol of hate-filled protests. Just one social media post with a picture from Fiji and a question as to whether she was "unnatural," and she'd spent weeks dealing with spray-painted doors and windows, being shunned by her friends and family and losing two lucrative movie contracts. She'd been physically attacked twice, only surviving thanks to some very expensive bodyguards. Had it not been for Rahul and their wedding announcement, she would've been killed for sure. There was no point in telling Mia all this. Saira had sent her countless emails explaining, pleading, begging for understanding. All unanswered.

Saira took a sip of her mojito, then pushed the glass away. It was too sweet and not minty enough. She locked eyes with Mia. "It was so easy for you to ask me to give up my life. But what if I'd asked you to do the same? What if I'd asked you to leave your Hollywood life and come to Bollywood with me?"

"It's not the same." Mia's expression was inscrutable. "You can have a career, a life here. I don't speak any of the Indian languages. I wouldn't be able to get a job and I'd stick out like a sore thumb being a white woman."

"None of that affects me because America is so welcoming of brown people," Saira said, bitterness creeping into her voice. No matter how much she romanticized their past, there was a reason it hadn't worked out. Saira had to deal with obstacles and expectations that Mia couldn't even begin to understand, yet Mia had expected her to give up everything without being willing to do the same in return.

Mia was back to studying the menu and Saira did the same. *What was I thinking?*

Until this morning, she'd thought she could handle seeing Mia. She'd almost convinced herself that she'd idealized their month in Fiji, and that the years had dampened the intensity of her emotions. But now, sitting with Mia, Saira's heart pounded uncontrollably. Ten years ago they'd both been young and carefree, unencumbered by the grind of daily life and lost in the magic of their romance. Sometimes she pretended it had all been a beautiful dream. But now, in Mia's presence, it felt all too real.

Saira hoped that apologizing to Mia, explaining why she'd broken up with her in such a heartless way would ease the restlessness in her heart. That closure on their relationship would finally let her move on, focus on what was really important, securing her future. But Mia still got under her skin. Mia with her irritating habit of sucking down ice-cold drinks, Mia with her half smiles and hazel eyes that looked green in the light and brown in the dark. It wasn't closure that she needed. It was Mia.

The waitress finally made her way to their

table, placing a fresh glass of Diet Coke in front of Mia.

"I'll have the pork pad-see-ew," Mia said, then gave her a small smile. "I still order that every time."

Saira's heart fluttered. The waitress looked at her expectantly, and she couldn't remember what she wanted to order. "I'll have the same, thank you." She handed the menu to the waitress.

Mia took a long draw from her drink. "Look, I know working together is going to be complicated, but I want to bury the hatchet. I don't want to talk about Fiji. I've worked very hard to forget about it. What do you need me to say so we can move on from that?"

I want you to tell me that you haven't stopped thinking about me in the last ten years, just as I haven't stopped thinking about you. I want you to tell me that seeing me again is messing with your head, just as it is mine. I want you to tell me that you forgive me.

"You're right. We should put the past behind us and focus on the show." If Mia wanted to leave the past behind, Saira would do her best to follow suit. *It's for the best.* She couldn't spend the next twelve weeks pining for what could have been. She needed to focus on what should be—her work, her future.

Maybe, just maybe, if she threw herself into her work, she could forget about Mia and move on with her life.

Four

Mia hated table reads. The one for *Life with Meera* promised to be an extra level of torture. Normally a read through this late in the production stage was designed to sharpen or fine-tune the dialogue. Peter had said they'd had one several weeks ago with Saira on Zoom. She hadn't been able to fly over because of her filming schedule in India. This read through was just to get Saira comfortable with the rest of the actors—a formality.

They were set up in a conference room, eight tables organized in a hollow square. There were sixteen actors for the show, with only five that had major roles. Mia began rearranging the tent cards that Gail had placed just moments earlier.

"Now I'm going to have to move the scripts," Gail moaned.

"Saira needs to be in the middle of the crowd, not at the head of the table."

"You do know she's the star?" Gail said. "And that this is a hollow square. There isn't really a head of table."

Mia picked up Saira's tent card and put her in an off-center seat near the corner. "Trust me—no one will need reminding that she's the star."

It was the first time everyone on the show would get to see Mia in action. How she dealt with Saira would determine their on-set dynamic for the next twelve weeks.

"What is your history with her?"

Mia avoided Gail's gaze. Her friend had a way of being able to tell when Mia was lying. "It's not important. We ran into each other ten years ago, and let's just say that she didn't leave the best impression on me."

Mia felt a twinge of guilt not telling Gail the full story. It wasn't as if they didn't talk about their love lives.

"Is working with her going to be a problem?"

Mia lifted her eyes and met Gail's look of worry. "There will be no problem. I know how to handle Saira."

"What if she knows how to handle you?"

Mia turned away. How well did Saira know her? *About as well as you know her.* She finished moving the name cards and stepped back to survey the table. Saira knew the old Mia. The one whose heart was open, the one who used to believe in peace and love and happily ever after. That Mia was long gone.

"Did you hear about George Valencia?" Gail chatted as they rearranged the scripts.

Mia shook her head. There was too much la-la land gossip to keep up with. She could count on Gail to keep her posted with whatever was relevant.

Gail stopped what she was doing and faced Mia dramatically. "His wife outed him last night at the Netflix party."

"Excuse me?"

"Yeah, they've been married for like ten

years, and Tracey said they're getting a divorce because he's gay."

Mia shook her head. Relationships were messy but she'd worked with George. He was a nice guy. He didn't deserve to be publicly humiliated.

"That's not really nice of her to out him."

"It's not an amicable divorce, and she says he's been a hypocrite. He outwardly supports LGBTQ rights but won't come out because he's afraid it'll affect his career."

"There's always an excuse. There are plenty of LGBTQ actors and actresses in LA. It's not even news when someone comes out anymore. Why do people want to live a lie? Sneaking around, not able to openly be in a relationship, hiding who you are. It's no way to live." Mia stopped before she said anything more. She wasn't just talking about George Valencia.

Mia had opened up to her parents about being lesbian in her last year of high school. She came from a religiously conservative Southern family and it hadn't gone well. Her father had raged, her mother cried. They tried to talk, cajole and threaten her into changing her mind about being gay. Finally, they kicked her out of the house. A friend's family took her in so she could finish high school, and as soon as she'd turned eighteen, she'd headed to LA and film school on financial aid.

"Well, this time George being outed is big news. It's all over social media. People are saying he's a hypocrite. He should have come out."

Mia slapped the last script on the table. "Why did he have to *come out*? Being sexually fluid is normal. What if we made everyone who is cis hetero come out and announce their sexuality?"

Gail stepped to her and put a hand on Mia's shoulder. "I didn't know you felt this strongly about it. I was just sharing news."

Mia softened. Who was she to judge anyway? She was a check writer where gay rights were concerned. She donated to organizations who worked on the ground level, but she didn't march, parade or attend protests.

"George Valencia being gay shouldn't have been a story. His wife shouldn't have been able to hold that over him and embarrass him by making an announcement."

Gail shrugged. "It's not a story because he's gay. It's a story because his show is on season ten, and his role is a seventies era mansplaining playboy. It's hard enough to renew a show once it gets to the double digits, but he's going to have a hard time convincing an audience that he's a lady killer."

Mia shook her head. "He's a talented actor who has convinced audiences for ten years that he can seduce women. The fact that his sexuality will affect his career is wrong. If the network doesn't renew, I hope he sues their asses."

"Have you ever been with a partner who was in the closet?"

Mia stiffened. Was Gail purposely asking about Saira? She shook the thought away. No one knew about her and Saira. It was too painful to talk about, so she didn't discuss it with anyone.

"Just once. That's why I don't date people who don't live their lives openly. The lying, the hiding, it all makes you feel like you're doing something wrong. The way we live our lives is not wrong. It shouldn't even be considered different."

"You know, you should join this group that the network…."

Mia held up a hand. "Please don't tell me to join a committee, working group or organization. That's another thing I disagree with. We shouldn't have separate committees to promote our rights. When we don't like the options from food services, we form a committee to tell them what they should serve. The more separate committees we have, the more we get othered. We should be part of every committee there is, we should be part of that stupid food services committee, telling them to serve rainbow sherbet. Instead, we're set aside in a committee of our own, madc to feel like we should be grateful for any concession we get."

Gail held up her hands. "Rainbow sherbet?"

Mia smiled. "Bad example. But you know what I mean."

"Sorry I brought it up. I didn't know you felt so angry about this. Actually, I don't even know what you're angry about, exactly."

Neither did Mia. This was Saira's fault. It was Saira who was reminding her of all the reasons why she didn't date women who were in the closet. It was Saira whose ability to set her body on fire with just a look was making her do bizarre things like rearrange seating so she didn't have to look directly at her. She wasn't angry with LGBTQ committees, and she didn't even care about George Valencia and his life. She was angry with Saira, the woman she had loved, the woman she had wanted to spend her life with, who had chosen to live a fake life with a real husband.

They heard noise outside the room; others were starting to arrive. Gail leaned over and spoke softly. "If it makes you feel any better, you know who won by the announcement? Ned Hawkins. Apparently he and George have been lovers for years.

Mia shook her head. "I'll bet you money that Ned didn't win anything. He's spent years being alone, unable to take his lover to parties or dinner openly. Now that George is finally out, there'll be such a spotlight on them that they won't even be able to enjoy it. Everyone loses."

Mia walked away to greet the first actors that started to file in. Some gave her a hug, others an elbow bump, and a few air kisses. They had a catering table set with fruit, bagels, avocado toast and little flutes filled with muesli. Some people grabbed coffee, a few nibbled at the table. Saira hadn't shown up and Mia was definitely not watching the door for her.

After their dinner the night before, Mia had spent the night thinking about whether she'd been too harsh on Saira about her fake marriage. She didn't know what it was like to be a celebrity, or to live in India, but Mia had sacrificed a lot to live her life openly. To this day, she was estranged from her parents.

Where was Saira anyway? Mia scanned the room and startled when she landed on Saira, in her assigned seat and studying the sheets in front of her. She was wearing a see-through white shirt with a flaming red bra-like undershirt that showed off her figure in that casually sexy way that sent heat waves coursing through Mia. *Damn that woman.*

Saira looked up suddenly and Mia instinctively looked away, realizing a second too late how childish the gesture was.

"Mia!"

She turned toward Gail. "Sorry, what were you saying?"

"Do you want to start?"

Mia nodded distractedly. The faster they were done with the read through, the sooner Saira with her red bra and see-through top would be out of her line of sight.

Gail called the meeting to order and explained the process. Mia began with a welcome speech, talking about how she was honored to have the job, big shoes to fill and the most talented staff on network television. It was the speech every producer gave, and everyone nodded politely. Then the director, David, had to say his piece. Finally, they began.

The read through started off well. Everyone was perfectly timed, effortlessly dialoguing like a team of champion synchronized swimmers. Saira was brilliant, her tone and accent pitch-perfect.

They got through the opening scene and

took a break. Mia began to relax and walked over to the catering table to grab a muffin.

"I see lemon poppyseed is still your go-to."

Mia closed her eyes for a second before turning to face Saira. "Nice job in the read through. You've got the accent down."

"About that. I don't think Meera should have an American accent."

I knew things were going too well.

"Why not?"

"She was born in Mumbai and moved here as a teenager. She's going to have an Indian accent."

"The TV show is airing here. Strong accents don't do well with audiences. They want to understand the characters, see themselves in them."

"Then what differentiates this show from all the others? Why not cast some American actress?"

Mia blew out a breath. "There are plenty of American actresses that we can cast if you'd rather not play the role."

Saira narrowed her eyes. "You need me for this role. The network is banking on selling the show in foreign markets, and I am an international star. I want this show to be authentic, not the same bullshit this network usually puts out."

Mia crossed her arms, hugging herself to keep her temper in check.

"If you hate the network so much, why did you sign with us?"

"Because I was promised a different show, and I intend to make it happen."

She walked away, and Mia nearly shouted at her but stopped just in time. The other actors and crew were clearly pretending not to listen while straining for every word. Gossip on a set was like happy meals at McDonald's. Everyone wanted the special toy.

Mia pasted a smile on her face and made small talk with the other people milling around the coffeepot.

As soon as the second scene began, Mia knew it was going to be bad. Saira was saying her lines in her normal accent. Mia loved the sound of Saira's usual inflections. She had that upper-crust Indian accent that clearly enunciated each word. If Saira's co-actors were thrown off by the sudden accent change, they recovered quickly.

Mia waited until the end of the scene before speaking up. "That was good, but I don't think the accent is working, Saira. Let's go back to the one you used for scene 1." Mia congratulated herself on how calm and matter-of-fact her voice sounded. No trace of rage, frustration, or annoyance.

"I'd like to hear what the others think about the two accents," Saira said just as matter-of-factly. She gave Mia a thin smile and a hard look.

Gail spoke up first. "I think the American accent is more relatable."

"I like the Indian one—it fits better with the character." The actress playing Meera's boss spoke up. Mia dug her nails into her hands to keep from saying something she'd regret.

"Not saying that you don't do the American accent well, but it sounds fake, y'know, I think the Indian one sounds better too," the actor playing Meera's best friend chimed in.

"I think we should consider it," David, the director, said.

Et tu, David? If there was one person Mia could count on to veto last-minute changes, it was David. He was a meticulous planner. If he thought this was a good idea, was Mia shooting it down just because it came from Saira? Mia mentally shook her head. She had considered the accent issue days ago, and after researching it and talking with the marketing people, she had agreed with Peter's original decision.

"Thanks for the input, everyone. Let's take an early lunch break while I listen to the recording." Mia dismissed the group. The lunch catering hadn't been set up so most of the group dispersed. Mia caught Saira just as she was about to leave.

"Can I have a word in my office, please."

They rode the elevators in silence. Once in her office, Mia shut the door.

"What's your plan, exactly?" Mia stood with her hands on her hips. She and Saira were nearly the same height when Saira wore her stiletto heels.

Saira met her gaze with a maddeningly serene expression on her face. "My plan is to make the best series possible. We have ten episodes to convince the audience that this show is worth additional seasons."

"Then why are you hell-bent on questioning every single thing. Yesterday it was wardrobe, today it's the accent. I already have the writers working overtime because of all the script changes you keep requesting."

"I am not going to make a show that embarrasses me, and my culture. I don't want to be one more Indian actress who fakes an American accent and makes fun of the traditions I hold dear to my heart." Her lips quivered and Mia's heart stopped. There was something else going on with Saira. This was about more than just the show.

Mia relaxed her posture. "I admit that there are stereotypes in the script. Had I been involved from the beginning, I would've done some things differently. But we have to make the show palatable to American audiences. This isn't the BBC or a cultural documentary. It's a dramedy, and we need to make things extreme and funny for it to work."

"I get that. What you don't understand is that the show crosses lines I'm not willing to cross."

Mia sighed. She was tired, out of words to

reason with Saira and too distracted by the way her jeans hugged her legs. Not to mention that damn red bra.

"Then quit," she said wearily.

"Is that really what you want me to do?"

No! I want you to behave. If Saira really did quit the show, it would be a disaster. They couldn't replace her quickly, the filming would have to be delayed and there was a good chance the network would just scrap the show. Then Mia would be back to making low-budget, limited series that nobody watched.

Saira stepped toward her. "What's really the matter Mia? Are you having trouble working with me."

Yes. You're driving me crazy—reminding me of our time in Fiji, making me lose sleep because I spent all night thinking about you.

Meeting Saira's gaze, Mia lifted her chin. "The only problem I have working with you is that you think your way is always the right way."

Saira scoffed. "Excuse me? You're the one who's so fixated on maintaining control over our relationship that you're not even willing to consider my suggestions. Do you know how hard it was for me to get you on this show? My agent called in every favor he had just to make it happen."

Mia's heart sank as she took in Saira's's words. She had assumed that the network had chosen her based on merit. "What do you mean your agent called in favors to get me this show?" Mia's voice trembled as she spoke.

Saira moved closer to her. "I thought you knew. When I heard Peter was leaving, I had my agent call everyone he knew at the network to get you the job."

"Why would you do that?" Even as disappointment sank in, Mia's heart perked up. Had Saira orchestrated their working together because she wanted to rekindle their relationship?

"Because I thought you'd understand my point of view. That you and I could make a good show."

Mia pressed her lips. "You thought you could manipulate me, that you could walk all over me and I'd let you."

Saira's eyes flashed, then she stepped close

and lowered her voice. "When have you ever let me have my way with you? If I remember correctly, you were always the one in charge."

Mia's face went hot. She had always been the one to take charge in bed, mostly because Saira had been inexperienced and tentative. But that didn't mean Saira was passive by any means. Heat spread through her as she remembered the way Saira would brush her lips against Mia's earlobes, kiss the crook of her neck, cup her breasts and pinch her nipples with just enough pressure to make Mia growl with need. "As I recall, you knew exactly what to do to get what you wanted."

Saira's lips twitched. "I had an excellent teacher, who was quite a seductress herself."

Mia's body tensed as Saira stepped even closer to her. She smelled the same, of roses and patchouli, her lips still glossed with the faintest shade of pink. As Saira's lips parted, all rational thought left Mia's brain. All she wanted was to once again feel the heat of Saira's mouth on hers, to feel the crush of her soft breasts against her own.

It was Saira who closed the distance between them, putting a hand on the back of Mia's head to pull their bodies closer together. As Saira's lips tugged and teased her mouth, Mia ran her hand up Saira's shirt. The feel of her soft, silky skin sent waves of heat coursing through her body. She ran her hand underneath the red top. As she'd suspected, Saira wasn't wearing a bra underneath that thing. Mia ran her thumb over Saira's hardened nipples and her own core pulsed with excitement as Saira moaned sinfully and deepened their kiss.

It was the sound of her office phone ringing that brought Mia back to her senses. No one ever used the landline, and Mia was unaccustomed to its shrill tone. *What am I doing?* Even as her brain kicked in, her hand lingered for another second on Saira's breast before she extracted her hand and disconnected her mouth.

She couldn't even look at Saira. If she did, there was no way any of her neurons would work. How could she have given in to the temptation to kiss her? As if their relationship wasn't complicated enough. Why had they even come to her office?

She answered the phone. It was Gail calling. Mia had left her cell phone in the conference room. She glanced at Saira, who was adjusting her shirt, putting her breasts back into the red top. Mia looked away before the urge to rip the damn thing overtook all rational thought.

She needn't have worried. What Gail had to say worked better than a cold shower. She hung up the phone and turned to Saira.

"Mia, we still..."

"Your husband is here. He wants to see you."

Five

As usual Rahul had the worst timing. The look on Mia's face had been clear as day. She was equal parts disgusted and furious. Whether it was with herself or with Saira, she didn't know. Saira could still feel the pressure of Mia's hands on her breasts, the touch of her lips and the heat of her skin. Mia had been so cold, Saira had wondered how she didn't feel the attraction that had been consuming Saira from the second she'd seen her in the dressing room. She had no doubts now. Part of what they had in Fiji was still alive.

Rahul had a crowd around him in the

white marble lobby of the studio building. Of course he did. He was a better known star than her. He'd even acted in several North American streaming TV series. It had been his contacts that had helped her land *Life with Meera.* He wore an untucked Nehru collar printed shirt in cream and gray with straight jeans that made him look like he had legs for days. Every hair on his head was styled and sprayed perfectly to look like he'd just gotten out of bed. As soon as he saw her, he broke through his fan girls and enveloped her in a bear hug, lifting her up. She returned his hug with equal gusto. It wasn't for show. They were truly the best of friends, and despite his timing, she was glad to see him. It would be good to have someone to talk to about Mia.

"What are you doing here?" she breathed. Rahul was the extreme opposite of a homebody. He hated being at home, so whenever he had a free moment, he used his private jet subscription to be someplace else. Saira would have a hard time coming up with a corner of the world where he didn't have an Instagram post.

"I missed you, *yaar*."

"I've only been gone two days."

"Too much for me." He pressed a kiss to her mouth, making sure it was long enough for cell phone pictures to capture the moment and share live on social media. Saira smiled dreamily at him, her acting skills in full use. She took him by the hand. "We have a small break—my hotel is nearby." She made sure her words were soft enough to seem secret but loud enough to be heard.

They walked out of the studio and she hailed a pedicab. The hotel was only two blocks away but she didn't feel like walking in heels. Plus, the driver wouldn't be able to hear what they were saying over the exertion of towing them on a bicycle and the noise of the city.

As soon as they were seated, Rahul waved to the fans as if they were in a royal carriage.

"Who did they catch you with this time?"

He sighed. "Hosiang. I thought we had equal reason to keep it quiet, but he had a crisis of conscience and told an elder. It spiraled from there."

Saira shook her head. "When will you

learn?" It was the one thing she and Rahul constantly argued about. Rahul fell in love with the frequency of a tweet, and every time he did, he got careless.

"C'mon, *yaar*, he's a monk and we've been seeing each other for months. How was I to know..."

"To know what? That he may eventually question whether he wanted to continue down a spiritual path or a hedonistic one? To think for a minute that any normal human being might go talk to a friend when faced with a major life choice, and that friend might knowingly or unknowingly betray them?"

His tanned skin paled. Rahul had been her best friend since they were four years old. They had grown up in the same apartment building in the Bandra section of Mumbai, a complex with high gates, strong security and easy access to the Bollywood studios. They were not allowed to leave the complex so they played in the hallways and at each other's homes. Saira knew before Rahul did that he was gay, just as he likely knew before her that she was. He'd been the one she'd called from Fiji, torn about Mia, panicked when their time together was ending. He'd meant well and thought he knew what was best for her, so he'd involved her parents. She had long forgiven him and hadn't brought it up in years, but seeing Mia had reopened old wounds. If only Rahul hadn't been so impetuous, she and Mia would have had a proper goodbye. Things would have ended differently. And maybe there was a small chance they would've found a way to be together all these years.

"Okay, fine. I should have known better. Thank you, once again, for saving my ass. You know my new movie opens next week. The financiers have put a lot of money into making it a blockbuster hit and we can't afford a scandal right now."

"You know what would make the movie a guaranteed hit? You coming out as being gay. Think of the free publicity."

"Yeah, that's why you've come out, *nah*? The free publicity that'll result in boycotts of the movie, social media roasting, hate mail, death threats, protests at the theaters so even those who support LGBTQ rights will be afraid to go see it."

"If this TV series is a success, then I am coming out."

He looked at her skeptically as their pedicab pulled up to the hotel. They made it to her room without being accosted, and in silence. Both had learned the hard way that hallway and elevator conversations were recorded on CCTV, which the paparazzi always managed to get hold of.

As soon as the door closed behind them, Rahul rounded on her. "You said you would come out if your last movie was a hit. As I recall, it was a blockbuster. So what happened?"

She stuck out her tongue. He looked around the small living room space of the suite, then made his way to the bedroom, plopped onto the bed and grabbed the TV remote. "My publicist says I just need to hang with you for the next couple of days. He's sending some local fans to put out posts. It'll be good for your show too."

He flipped through the TV channels. "This is a real third-rate hotel—no international sports channel. India is playing Sri Lanka in cricket."

Saira sat on the bed next to him and grabbed the remote, turning off the TV. "Your timing is really bad. Things with Mia have been tense."

He sat up. "Did you tell her about our marriage?"

"Yes. But I didn't tell her about you."

He took her hand and kissed it. "We'll figure it out. One day, we will find a way to live the way we want."

She squeezed his hand. "What did Hosiang decide?"

"He picked spirituality over hedonism. We broke up."

He put his head on her shoulder and she touched his cheek. Rahul sighed. "I can't even blame him. What can I offer him? A life of stolen kisses and hidden apartments. He has a life of enlightenment ahead of him."

"He has a life of dreaming about you ahead of him. In the beginning he will miss you and wonder whether he made the right decision. Then he'll get back into the routine of daily life and think all is fine. But every few days, something will happen to remind him of you. A scent, a song, a place. Each time that happens, it will tear his heart just a little. Bit by bit, those little tears are going to create a hole so deep in his heart that he won't even know how to fix it."

Rahul lifted his head and enveloped her in his arms. "Babe, you need to tell Mia how you feel."

"What do I tell her? That I've been pining for her for the last ten years? That all the other women I've been with paled in comparison to her? That I was hoping seeing her again would magically cure me of my obsession, but it's only made it worse?"

"That's exactly what you tell her."

"Then her next question will be, 'what do you want from me?'. What will I tell her? I don't know. If the show is a hit, maybe I'll move to LA and make a career in Hollywood. Then I'll come out to the world and hope that I can make a living here. Then she'll ask what happens if the show tanks."

"What do you plan to do if the show tanks?"

Saira sighed. If she knew the answer to that question, she would have Mia in her bed right now instead of Rahul.

"I kissed her today."

Rahul raised his brows. "I thought the plan was to focus on the show and slowly rekindle things with Mia."

"That was the plan. But…" Saira buried her face in her hands. "I didn't realize how hard it would be to…"

"To keep your hands off her? To be so close and yet not touch her?"

Rahul put his arm around her and squeezed her tight against his chest. "I know. Can I give you some advice?"

"As if I could stop you."

"The more you withhold, the harder it will get. Give in to temptation. Be with Mia, see what happens. The last time you guys were together, it was ten years ago. You were on vacation. See if what you had there can exist in the real world."

That's what she was afraid of. "What if it is real? Then what? I can't leave her again. What will I do if the show tanks?"

"Worst-case scenario. You come out and

ruin your Bollywood career, and you have no working options in Mumbai. You can live off your savings for years until you figure out something else. But the more likely scenario is that you'll still get some work. There are plenty of streaming channels that'll give you a chance— it might not be the lead, and you may have to reduce the number of Hermes scarves you buy on a weekly basis, but it's not like you'll starve."

Saira shook her head. "It's not about having nice things. You know I pay for Kayra's care. She likes the place in Switzerland but that costs a bucketload. If I come out, I'll have to pay for security for my parents. They are never leaving India."

"What happened to your savings? Your last few movies did really well."

"The rupee is really weak, paying for Kayra's surgeries and rehabilitation, then Jai's MBA at Harvard, and Ma's therapies have sucked up most of what I've made."

Rahul shook his head. "Your family is taking advantage of you. Kayra can move someplace cheaper, Jai should pay you back now that he has a job, and your Ma does not need her army of astrologers, pandits, yogis, and she definitely does not need those month-long ashram visits in Rishikesh."

Rahul was right. Saira recognized her family's excesses, but it also gave her joy to be able to provide those for them. Her mother's Bollywood career had ended early, and her father hadn't really been able to hold down a job. The family had only kept their home because of Saira's acting career. Saira wasn't just risking her own life, but that of her entire family.

"It's my fault Kayra is in that center. I'm not going to make her move someplace cheaper."

Rahul shook his head. "When will you stop blaming yourself? There was no way for you to have known what would happen."

"She never wanted to do it. I put her up to it. And you know why? Because I wanted more time for fun. I was tired of working and thought if Kayra had a career like mine, then it would take the pressure off me."

Rahul sighed. "You were a child!" He sat up suddenly. "You know, we don't have a prenup. If we divorce, you can take me for all I'm worth."

She shook her head. "I will not take money from you. I'll accept a guest room in one of your apartments when I'm homeless though." She bit her lip. "If I come out, what'll happen to you?"

He shrugged. "I'll have to find a hot model to have an affair with to drown my sorrows. I'm sure my publicist will spin it into something that makes me look like a hero or a raunchy horndog doing threesomes. I'll be fine. You've done more than enough for me. I should not be part of your calculation."

She gave him a hug. Rahul was the one person who not only understood her but actually cared for her.

"Saira, you're stressing over things you have no control over. Whether the show does well or not is not something you can control right now. But, finding out whether you and Mia can make it work is in your power. So stop sitting around playing what-if scenarios in your head. Go get your girl."

Six

Mia paced the floor of her office. *What is wrong with me?!* She had asked to speak to Saira in her office to address the accent issue. Instead, she'd ended up kissing her, and now Saira was off for a nooner with her husband and she was left to figure out how she was going to get their read through back on track. Lunch was ready, Gail had sent out a text message to everyone and the only person missing was Saira. Gail had dispatched an intern to Saira's hotel.

What bothered Mia most was that she wasn't sure whether she was more upset about Saira's behavior at the read through or her running off to her hotel room with her husband. Mia had always known that Saira's sexuality was more fluid than her own. She didn't for one second believe that her relationship with Rahul was completely platonic. They might be friends, they might even have an open marriage but Rahul was too sexy and Saira was too hot-blooded. How could she have run off with Rahul seconds after kissing Mia with such passion?

Mia took some deep breaths and rubbed her temples. *Focus on work.* It was the only thing that made sense right now. The only part of the whole mess with Saira that she could control, or at least try to.

She shook her shoulders, then made her way to the conference room. Most people were sitting down with their lunches. Food services had set up an extravagant spread, including ten different types of sandwiches ranging from vegan to double meat, smoothies and green juices in little cups, pasta salad (vegan and regular), three different types of green salads, a quinoa salad, a couscous salad, and two meats and cheeses charcuterie boards. Mia heaped her plate. She knew how much the food cost. If she had her way, they would have leftovers for the afternoon snack and dinner.

"Loading up for dinner?"

She nearly jumped out of her skin as Saira's breath caressed her ear.

"Where were you?" Mia cringed at the nagging inflection of her voice. *This is my show. Saira works for me.*

"Sorry for not seeing the text messages. My phone was on silent."

"You're here now. Had a good time with Rahul?"

Saira's lips twitched. She leaned forward, her lips brushing Mia's as she whispered. "Are you jealous we didn't finish what we started in your office?"

Mia's face heated. *How dare she!* She cleared her throat. "Actually I wanted a second with you to discuss the issue of the accent you'll be using." At least her voice had returned to normal.

Saira straightened. "Look, I understand your and the network's concerns about accents. You want to cater to an American audience and make sure that people won't lose interest in the show because they're having a hard time understanding the main character. Also, you want them to be able to relate to me, and it's hard to do that with someone who has an accent."

Mia stared at her. *Where is this rational side coming from?* The Saira she knew in Fiji was intractably stubborn. Once, they had planned to take a hike to see a waterfall. The locals had waved them away when they'd gotten near the top of the viewing hill, saying the rains the night before had made the trek too muddy. Saira had literally dug her heels in and made them trudge forward anyway.

Saira placed a hand on her arm. Mia ignored the warmth of her touch. "How about if we go halfway. I won't talk like I normally do, but I won't go all American either. That way the character authentically has an Indian accent but it won't be so strong that the audience won't like it."

Mia sighed.

"Let's try it out with the next scene and see how you like it." Saira's tone was so reasonable that Mia found herself nodding.

They started the read through of the next scene, and Mia marveled at Saira's ability to effortlessly change her accent once again. They took a short break, then started the next scene.

"Saira, I want to you to read this scene in your normal accent," Mia said.

Saira raised her brows but didn't say anything. Mia hated to admit it, but Saira had been right. The dialogue worked better with her precise pronunciation and slightly musical way of stringing words together. It was charming.

Gail slid a note to her that said "good call." Mia gave her a sideways look.

It was evening by the time they finished. Mia had set an early morning call for taping. The first season wouldn't be filmed in front of a live audience so they had the flexibility of being able to start early. The filming schedule was aggressive—they were taping ten episodes in sixty working days for an average of three days per episode. It was one of the hardest schedules that Mia had worked with. Mia finished the day with a pep talk to the actors and crew, promising an amazing wrap-up party when they got through the next three months. Fighting for as much time as possible was one of the many things she'd had to negotiate with the network. The brutal schedule was necessary to make sure the series could air in February, and her ability to deliver would make her career. On the other hand, if there were significant delays, no one would remember what an impossible schedule she'd had. She would simply be blamed for not being able to cut it.

Most of the actors escaped as soon as Mia was done with her instructions and wrap-up. Some lingered and socialized with each other and the crew. Mia checked in with key crew members, making sure they were ready for the next day. TV series always made it seem as though actors messing up their lines was what took so long on set but the truth was that a lot of time was spent in scene transitions, changing camera positions and a myriad of other back-end tasks. Mia had tried to minimize those as much as possible so they could transition more easily between scenes. Tomorrow would be a test of whether all her planning would work. A lot depended on Saira. If she kept requesting changes, they would fall behind, and with a schedule so tight, they had no wiggle room.

"You hate chitchat." Mia closed her eyes. How did Saira manage to sneak up to her?

"I'm not socializing. I'm making sure we're ready for tomorrow."

Saira gave her a smile. "This is the most organized set I've ever been on. I'm sure everything will go smoothly."

The compliment warmed Mia more than she wanted to admit. She didn't need Saira's approval. But she did need her cooperation. "Saira, listen, I know we've gotten off on the wrong foot with this show, but I want you to know that I am willing to listen to your suggestions. The taping schedule is just really tight, so if something will delay us, I can't do it."

Saira bit her lip.

Shit. I know what that means. Saira was going to say something that Mia wasn't going to like.

"I know the taping schedule is fast. My agent even tried to negotiate on it because it takes us double, triple, the time to tape for the same number of minutes in India."

"It takes double the time here too. That's what makes this schedule so aggressive. But we can do it because I know how talented you are, and I think we can do it in fewer takes."

Saira smiled. "Flattery will get you everywhere..."

But...

"...but getting this show right is important to me." She held out the paper script and Mia recoiled. "After the read through today, I have some additional suggestions. The script was stilted in some sections, especially if we aren't using my American accent, there are ways of saying thing in India that..."

"Saira! We're taping tomorrow. It's not fair to the other actors to change the script the night before."

Her stomach turned. Would she keep having the same argument over and over with Saira for the next three months? Mia wasn't a stranger to arguing with actors on set, but Saira wore her out. As much as she wanted to deny it, Mia couldn't ignore that there was still a physical and emotional connection between them. She hadn't forgotten Fiji and neither had Saira.

"I haven't changed anyone else's dialogue, just my own."

"Still. I have to go back to the writers, who are going to have to work well into the night. Then the script has to get approved. I need to make sure it won't require set design changes..."

"It doesn't require set design changes. You haven't even looked at my changes and you're already shutting me down. You still think of me as that naive woman you met in Fiji, but let me tell you..."

"Would you stop bringing up Fiji. What happened there was ten years ago. A lifetime. We are both different people now, and this show has nothing to do with Fiji."

Saira stepped toward her. Mia caught a whiff of Saira's perfume and her body responded immediately, her hands remembering the feel of Saira's skin, the way her nipples swelled and hardened under her touch. Her eyes dropped to Mia's lips, her own mouth remembering the kiss they shared just a few hours ago. It wouldn't take much for her to take a step and close the distance between them. Just one step and she could claim Saira's mouth, rip that stupid red top right off her breasts and feel those hard nipples in her mouth.

Saira leaned in to whisper, and Mia couldn't help the goose bumps on her arm as her warm breath caressed her .

"This show has everything to do with you and me, and we have everything to do with Fiji."

I can't do this.

Before she could formulate words in her head, Saira took her hand and pressed something that felt like a credit card into her palm.

"We can keep arguing or do what we want to do. You know where I'm staying. Come by after you're done with work tonight. Maybe we can finish what we started in your office."

Mia squeezed her hand shut, letting the hotel key dig into her palm. She turned away so she wouldn't watch Saira walk out. One night. That's all it would take to get Saira out of her system. Then maybe she could focus on the show instead of thinking about Saira, focus on what was between her ears instead of what was happening between her legs. Would it be so bad, to give in to temptation just this once? She and Saira never had a proper goodbye. Mia never had a last time with Saira. Maybe that's why she'd never been able to get Saira out of her system. What if she did that now? What if she had one night with Saira, knowing it would be their last time together? Could it provide the closure she needed?

"Have you seen the script changes Saira's requesting?"

Mia forced herself to look at Gail. She was holding the script that Saira had had in her hand just minutes ago.

"She mentioned them to me."

Gail sighed and fanned the pages, showing Mia a whole lot of red writing. "She's virtually rewritten every single one of her dialogues. The writers' room is going to be pissed."

They weren't the only ones. Mia pocketed the hotel room key and grabbed the pages. Saira's changes would throw the timing off.

The camera crew would need to retool; the other actors would need time to adjust to the new dialogue even if their lines weren't changed. Saira had no idea how her decision rippled through everyone around her.

"Tell her no," Mia said firmly.

"Didn't you see the email from Chris O'Toole?"

Mia sighed. "Now what?"

"Apparently, they signed a new contract with Saira this morning. I thought you knew about it. She's taking a fee cut in exchange for script approval."

Mia clenched her jaw. "I asked Chris to run the changes by me before they signed. But did our financial wiz of a network executive consider the downstream costs of these script changes? Or the potential delays to our filming schedule? No, he did not."

Gail put a hand on Mia's arm. "You know as well as I do that they can't see past the ends of their noses. But that's not our biggest problem. What the hell is going on between you and Saira? Are you two sleeping together?"

Mia recoiled. “What? Why would you ask me that question?”

“Because you can’t stop looking at each other, and then there’s the fact that she slipped you her hotel key card.”

Mia’s face heated. “There is nothing going on between us.”

Gail put her hands on her hips. “Really?”

Mia’s stomach knotted. She didn’t want Gail to know about her and Saira, but she couldn’t keep lying to her friend.

“Look, I told you we knew each other. The truth is that we were seeing each other for like a hot minute ten years ago when both of us were on vacation in Fiji.”

“Ten years ago?” Gail said skeptically.

Mia nodded. “It was just a fling, over a long time ago.” It was over. It had been for ten years. They hadn’t spoken or been together. Still, one day back and all the old feelings were coursing through her body like a tornado on a collision course with her heart.

“Clearly not.”

Mia changed the subject. “Let’s go over the script changes. And how much Chinese, pizza, and espresso we're going to have to buy the writers so they don't go on strike." She couldn't talk about Saira. Not with her emotions so raw, and the feel of Saira's mouth still tingling on her lips.

She and Gail found a spot on the conference room table. Everyone else had cleared out. They worked through Saira's script changes. Mia had to grudgingly admit that Saira's changes weren't all bad. Many of them made the dialogue more punchy. She recalled Saira's accusation that she hadn't been taking her suggestions seriously. She was right. Mia had been too focused on making sure that she set the tone for their relationship, that she remained in control and didn't let her feelings for Saira resurface. She had failed on all counts.

Gail gathered the script after they'd made their notes. "I'll get this to the writers' room. They won't be happy that Saira did a better job than them, but there isn't much for them to do other than proofing."

Mia reminded Gail to also send the script to the other actors and crew. Once Gail had left, she took out the hotel key that Saira had given her. It would be so much easier to give in to what they were both obviously feeling. Maybe it would take Saira off her mind. Maybe it would make her forget about Fiji. Maybe it would clear her mind of all the noise that had prevented her from being in a meaningful relationship all these years.

Or it would destroy her. They still had chemistry—the kiss proved it. What if sex was even better? Would Mia spend the next ten years comparing every woman to Saira? Her last relationship had lasted four months, two months longer than the one before. She was finally moving on, finding a way to open her heart and her body to others. But a part of her was still stuck on Saira.

She picked up the key. *I know what I have to do.*

Seven

"Would you please hurry up. Mia will freak if she sees you here."

"Going, going." Rahul gave his hair one last spray and set the bottle on the counter. Saira picked it up and put it in a shopping bag. She couldn't have Mia seeing Rahul's stuff all over the place. The hotel had been fully booked, so it was harder than she'd thought to get Rahul a room, let alone a room on the same floor so the paparazzi wouldn't find out that they were staying in separate rooms. Ultimately, Rahul had decided to go visit an old "friend" in Orange County, a B-list Hollywood actor. Rahul had a one-night stand with Ned Hawkins several years ago. They'd been friends since. Ned offered up his house to both Rahul and Saira, since he was leaving town the next day. Apparently, the media had made his life miserable after an announcement from his lover's wife about their affair. He'd decided to leave town and go hide in an undisclosed location.

Rahul washed his hands and dropped the towel on the floor. As much as Saira loved him, he was a slob. He was used to an army of servants in Mumbai who picked up after him. She put his things in shopping bags and handed it to the waiting bellhop. The sound bite to the media was that they were staying with Ned Hawkins. Saira was only using the hotel room provided by the studio on the nights she had an early call.

Just as she had him out the door, Rahul turned to her. "Tell her how you feel, babe. What have you got to lose?"

My dignity. She couldn't tell Mia how she felt. Not until she knew that Mia still felt *something* for her. There was a lot that she had to make up to Mia, and still a lot of things she needed to figure out. But the first thing to know was whether she and Mia still shared a bond. Saira couldn't give up her whole life on a chance that they could be together. She had to know for sure.

She looked at her watch. It had been two hours since she'd left the studio. She fluffed her hair, reapplied lip gloss, adjusted the silk slip she had put on. When three hours had passed, she sighed, plopped on the bed and opened her laptop to look at scripts. She had two agents, one who worked the Bollywood circuit and the other in Los Angeles. Both had sent her new projects. Mumbai was offering her a high-budget film with an all-star cast and her as Mumtaz Mahal, the wife of Shah Jahan, the emperor who had built the Taj Mahal. The movie was about their love story and how it inspired the building of one of the wonders of the world. The script was emotive and powerful, and she'd be working with one of the best directors and producers in Mumbai. They were also offering 2 percent over her usual asking price because they wanted her exclusively in Agra for filming. Her agent was sure he could get her 10 percent over her usual fee for exclusive access. If she signed the project, that would put her in India for at least nine months after filming for *Life with Meera* ended.

Crossing her fingers, she looked at what her Hollywood agent had come up with. There was a cameo appearance as herself in an A-list movie, a best friend supporting role in a rom-com that had literally put her to sleep as she read the script and a meeting with an online streaming network to discuss a six-episode limited series. None of these were paying half of what she'd be getting from Mumbai.

She opened the latest balance sheets her accountant emailed her on a weekly basis. The rupee was weak against global currencies, including the Swiss franc. Kayra's rehab center was costing her nearly 40 percent more than it had the previous year. She closed her eyes. Kayra was so happy there. How could she ask her to move? Then there were invoices for her mother's ashram. Her mother had struggled after what had happened with Kayra. Since she'd started going to the ashram, she seemed happier. How could Saira take that away from her?

Her LA publicist had sent some positive articles and social media posts from her kissy scenes with Rahul today. Her own arrival in LA had gone unnoticed but, as usual, Rahul's presence elevated her own exposure. Rahul had invitations to some high-profile Hollywood parties and her publicist told her in no uncertain terms that she needed to go, and listed out the invited celebrities with whom she should try and get pictures.

Saira sighed. She was essentially starting over in Hollywood, building her presence. In India she was already well-known. Crowds greeted her wherever she went, but she'd have to build her reputation here, get the media to love and promote her. Was she ready to put in that work all over again?

Her watch told her that four hours had passed. It was getting late. Mia wasn't coming. She took a deep breath, then emailed her Mumbai agent.

Mia turned the hotel key over in her hand. She was standing outside Saira's hotel.

"Are you ready to come in?"

Mia smiled politely at the valet/doorman/bellhop who had turned from eyeing her with suspicion to regarding her with pity. He'd seen the room key in her hand and probably, correctly, surmised that she was debating whether or not to compromise herself.

What if she and Saira were still as red-hot as they'd always been? What if they weren't'? She'd held the idea of Saira in her heart and head for so long that she wasn't even sure what was real versus imagined. Now was a good time to find out, wasn't it?

She looked at her watch. They had an early call in the morning. Saira needed her beauty sleep. Mia needed to be clearheaded.

According to the app on her phone, a rideshare driver was one minute away. She could be home in thirty minutes. Plenty of time to get eight hours of sleep. *Or I can sleep with Saira's naked body next to me.*

She took a deep breath, then stepped into the lobby.

When she got to the room door she paused. Should she knock or just use the key? What if Saira had changed her mind? She had passed a mirror in the hallway. Retreating her steps, she considered her appearance. She never wore much makeup, but would it have killed her to swipe some mascara on her lashes and gloss on her lips? She dug through her purse and came up with ChapStick. Something was better than nothing. She tugged down her T-shirt, then squared her shoulders.

She used the little doorbell and stood with her hands behind her back. As she waited, she crossed her arms, then moved them beside her, then in front. Why the hell couldn't she figure out what to do with the damned things. She was used to always having something in her hands: a laptop, iPad, clipboard, coffee cup. Why hadn't she thought of bringing a bottle of wine or something?

How many minutes had passed? She wasn't sure but it seemed like a lot. She rang the bell again. What if Saira wasn't there? What if she'd changed her mind? Then another thought struck her. Rahul! Was he there? What if the two of them were together? What if they were making love right now?

She turned and fled down the hall.

"Mia?"

She turned so fast that she nearly tripped and fell. Saira stood at the door. *Damn that woman.* She was wearing a cream-colored knee-length silk nightgown with no bra. The straps looked like they could barely hold the piece up. Her breasts swelled against the fabric, her hard nipples on full display. Her hair was tousled, as if she'd been asleep.

Mia closed the distance between them, grabbed Saira by the hair and kissed her hard. Saira returned the kiss with equal fervor, pulling her into the room and closing the door behind them. Mia had no control left. She squeezed Saira's breasts, enjoying the moan that escaped deep from her throat. She had Saira pinned against the hotel door. She moved her hands down Saira's waist and thighs, her own body heating and zinging with need as her hands touched Saira's soft skin. Normally Mia liked to take things slowly, enjoy the initial seduction—she got off on making her partners moan and writhe under her mouth and fingers—but tonight her body seemed to be possessed with an urgency she couldn't control.

She ran her hand between Saira's thighs. Saira bit her lip, bucked her hips in clear invitation. She wasn't wearing any panties, something Mia had expected but still found intensely arousing. Her own panties were wet with need but Mia pressed her thumb to Saira's clit, enjoying the way her body tensed and vibrated; her own body responded to the sinful moan from deep within Saira's throat. She slid one finger inside Saira, as deep as it would go, then pushed even deeper. Saira broke their kiss, bent her body, tightening against Mia's finger and burying her mouth in her neck, kissing her in that spot that drove her wild. Mia slid a second, then a third finger inside Saira, her own body pulsing, vibrating and aching with desire as Saira's moans turned into cries of ecstasy, and she clenched so tightly against Mia's fingers that for a second Mia worried they might break.

Just when Saira was close, Mia used her other hand to push the flimsy nightgown off one shoulder. Saira was more than happy to help. With her fingers still inside her, Mia sucked on Saira's nipple, its firmness and sweet taste nearly throwing Mia off the edge. She sucked hard, biting ever so slightly just as she felt Saira's orgasm shudder through her body. Saira screamed, dug her fingers into Mia's shoulders and bit her lip as she threw her head back. It was a while before her body relaxed and Mia slipped her fingers out, her own body so raked with need that she wasn't sure how she was still standing.

Saira grabbed her shirt and tugged it up, then deftly took off her bra. Not waiting for permission, Saira mouthed one hard nipple and ran her thumb over the other. Mia put her hands on Saira's now naked waist, enjoying the feel of her hot, silky skin. She closed her eyes, letting the waves of pleasure course through her. Saira dragged her into the bedroom, pushing her onto the bed, and Mia complied with no resistance. She helped Saira take off her cargo pants and panties and spread her legs to let her put her mouth on her hot core. Saira's tongue teased her clit, in turn flicking across it and pushing hard on it. She slipped two fingers inside Mia, bending and curving them until Mia was writhing on the bed, trying desperately to hold on to control. She didn't want to give in quite yet. Mia wanted to enjoy the moment, drag it out, let her body burst into flames. But Saira was relentless. She put a third finger inside Mia, sucked hard on her clit, and just when Mia was on the edge, she withdrew her fingers, stuck her thumb inside, bending it just right. Mia's entire body pulsed, then convulsed and bucked so hard that she nearly threw Saira off-balance. Her orgasm was explosive, and Saira teased and caressed her with her mouth and fingers until Mia begged her to stop. When she was finally spent, Saira crawled on top of her and buried her face in Mia's chest. Their cores, still hot and eager, rubbed and melted together.

It was good to have Mia underneath her. Her body was warm and soft and solid all at the same time. She could hear Mia's heart thudding, and the sound was like a soothing balm on her chaotic soul. They were meant to be together. If she had any doubts about that, they had evaporated. Nothing had changed in the last ten years, they still had what they had in Fiji: love, passion and a future together. This time she was ready to do what was needed to make it happen. Mia was worth it. Saira would find a way to get work in Hollywood. She could move her entire family to America to keep them safe from public retribution. She would find Kayra a place that was cheaper and that she loved just as much. Maybe Kayra was even ready to come home. Saira would figure it out. For Mia, Saira would make it work.

Mia shifted beneath her and Saira lifted her head, her body moving instinctively so that their breasts crushed together, their hardened nipples rubbed against each other. Saira pushed her hips to rub against Mia. She was ready for round two, aching for it. Her body pulsed with need, her core slick and ready.

"Saira." Mia's voice was thick.

Saira put a hand between their legs and caressed Mia, enjoying the way her eyes closed. She was just as ready as Mia was. Saira lifted herself and rolled off Mia so she could reach the nightstand. She had all of Mia's favorite toys ready; there was no need for sleep tonight. Saira had spent the last ten years reliving Fiji, imagining this night. They would make love again and again, and in between they would talk about the future, but this time with the maturity to actually make it happen.

She had barely gotten the drawer open when Mia rolled off the bed. "Toilet or shower? If it's the latter, then I'll join you."

Mia wouldn't look at her. She walked around the bed and began collecting her clothes. Saira tensed, her heart racing, and not in the way that she wanted it to.

"What're you doing?"

Mia wouldn't answer, wouldn't look at her. She jerked into her underwear and cargo pants. Saira rolled off the bed. Mia slipped her shirt on top of her head and pocketed her bra.

No, no no no. This can't be happening. Saira placed her hands on Mia's shoulders.

"Mia, talk to me. What's going on. Why are you leaving?"

Mia still wouldn't look at her, so Saira bent

her head and placed a featherlight kiss on her lips. She wrapped her arms around Mia's waist. "Babes, let's talk. Tell me what's going on. You can't just leave like this. We have the whole night ahead of us. There are so many things for us to talk about—" then, unable to resist, she wiggled her eyebrows "…—so many things still to do."

Mia reached behind her waist and unlocked Saira's arms. She took a step back and finally met her eyes. "You wanted one night. I needed to get you out of my system. Now that's it's done, we can go back to focusing on the show."

Saira sat down on the bed. She didn't trust her legs to hold her. Tears stung her eyes. "This was just a roll in the bed for you?"

Mia nodded firmly. "We never had goodbye sex. Consider this closure on our past relationship."

Closure. What a filthy, American term. As if there was a way to seal closed a gaping open wound, as if mind-blowing, life-changing passion could be zipped up and put away like a winter blanket that was no longer needed in the summer.

Mia was slipping on her shoes. Saira placed a hand on her shoulder. “Mia, you can’t leave like this. We need to talk. Tonight wasn’t just meaningless sex.”

Mia turned to her with eyes blazing. “That’s exactly what it was for me, Saira. I’m not denying that we still have chemistry. Maybe now that we have it out of our system, we can move on, focus on the show. Be professional.”

Saira stepped back. “That’s all you care about? The show?”

Mia nodded. “That is the only thing I care about. You and I were over ten years ago. Clearly our libidos needed one last romp. Now, let’s move on and stop dwelling on the past.”

With that, she walked away, leaving Saira bewildered and shattered.

Eight

Mia rubbed her eyes, hoping it would take away the dark circles and bags that betrayed the sleepless night she'd had. *Damn Saira.* Mia had hoped that once they actually gave in to their desires, it would be clear that what they had was in the past. Mia had gotten together with exes before; it was never as good as she remembered it. Mia was convinced that she'd built up a fantasy-like utopia when it came to sex with Saira and a reality check would help her move on. Except it backfired. The reality was even better than her memory.

She'd come home to her crappy apartment

and spent the night reliving every moment with Saira, writhing with want and need. Her fingers and vibrator had both been useless, and now she was sleep-deprived, cranky and had the female version of blue balls.

Her watch chimed, letting her know it was time to leave. She swore, slipped on her shoes, grabbed her laptop bag and crossed her fingers that the coffee cart outside the studios was open. The damned thing opened and closed at the whim of its owner, a surfer whose schedule varied based on how good the waves were.

The way the universe was dumping on her, she wasn't surprised that the coffee cart wasn't open. She grabbed the sludge that the interns brewed in the common kitchen, then walked over to the studio where the series set had been built. She'd checked it the night before to make sure that the set design looked good. The studio was a hub of activity. The actors weren't due for another hour, but the camera crew, director and myriad other support staff had been there for a while. The director, David Rosen, was a thin, reedy man with a permanent scowl and glasses that Mia was sure were for aesthetics only. He was another source of heartburn for Mia because he was yet another control freak. But he knew how to do his job. The cameras were already positioned for the first shot, everyone knew what they needed to do and even the couch cushions were fluffed.

David strode over to her. "Script changes the night before. On this taping schedule!"

"Good morning to you too, David," Mia said evenly. "You know as well as I do that script changes happen even after the scene is filmed. What's the big deal?"

"The big deal is that it throws off the timings for my camera crew. I had to call them in an hour early to go over things. You're going to have to pay the overtime."

Great.

"Thank you for making it work, David. You know the deal the network made with Saira."

David leaned forward, his tone completely changed. "What is up with that? Is she sleeping with Chris?"

Mia stiffened. "I don't think so. She reduced her fee, and as usual, they don't always comprehend what that might mean for us on the ground level."

David nodded. "On my last show, they fired the producer halfway through filming because the actors complained about him. I had to do the directing and producing."

Mia bit the inside of her cheek. She was used to men like David. "Well, then you know exactly what a tough position I'm in. Thanks for being so great, David."

Without waiting for him to respond, she walked away. She could only take so much. Gail appeared with a dry cappuccino, and she took the cup gratefully.

"Everything ready?"

Gail nodded. "Saira's already here and sitting in makeup."

Saira, the woman who claimed that Indian Standard Time was genetic and responsible for her chronic lateness, was almost an hour early?

"She said her hair takes a while, and she wanted to make sure we started on time this morning. Got off to an auspicious start and all."

"How thoughtful," Mia said sarcastically.

Saira was up to something. Was she hoping to talk to Mia? Convince her to come to her dressing room for a noon romp? Mia's traitorous body pulsed at the very thought. She took a long sip of her hot cappuccino, letting it burn her mouth.

If Saira had her way, the script for their romance was written clearly in Mia's mind. They would spend three months stealing every second they could get, quickies in the dressing room, nights filled with unbridled passion, innuendo laden looks and gestures throughout the day. Saira would talk about the future, plans to move to LA, to start a new career and live with Mia out in the open. She would even go as far as to drag Mia to look at houses she would buy for them to live together. A two-bedroom house in the hills, above the smog. They would commute to the studios together—it was worth it for the view. Then as the show wrapped, Saira would get distant. The small house she was going to rent or buy would no longer be available. The contracts she was sure were coming wouldn't materialize. There was an excellent offer from Bollywood that

Saira couldn't refuse. It would just be a few months, then Saira would come back. At the wrap-up party, Saira would say goodbye to everyone but Mia, promising that she would return the next weekend on a friend's private jet. It was just a few months and then Saira's Hollywood gigs would come through.

The weekend trip wouldn't materialize. The taping schedule, jet lag, a million excuses. Weeks would turn into months, and daily video calls would become emails and text messages until Saira would finally break down and admit that she couldn't make it work. She had too many responsibilities.

The truth that Saira would never admit, even to herself, was that she was afraid to leave the security of her life in India. She liked being a beloved film star where fans swooned at her every move. Directors and producers capitulated to her demands, an army of servants made sure she didn't even have to tie her own shoelaces. Why would she trade that to become a bottom list star in Hollywood where she'd have to beg or manipulate to get what she wanted and deal with the fact that her career was on the down slope?

It could never work between them. Saira wasn't suited to be an American. She would forever blame and resent Mia for making her give up a life she loved.

Mia passed by the makeup area, eyes on her iPhone, walking with purpose. She stole a glance only to see Saira's eyes on her. She gave Saira what she hoped was a nonchalant nod. Just another actress. Today was the director's show. Mia was there to make sure it all went smoothly. Saira was David's problem today, and the thought eased the knot in Mia's stomach.

The actors took their places for the first scene. It was based in the living room of the set. Saira was wearing pajamas. A set of plaid pajamas and a T-shirt that read I Love New York would've looked drab on anyone else, but it seemed to hug Saira in all the right places, giving her that girl next door combined with sexy porn star look. Mia couldn't help but stare.

The first few scenes went smoothly. The actors adjusted to the change in Saira's lines, and Mia stood mesmerized as she watched Saira act. She had seen Saira's Bollywood movies, with subtitles on. There was no doubt that Saira was a talented actress, but it was something else to watch her live. Rarely were actors able to get a scene perfect in one take. It was even rarer for directors to accept one cut. They wanted to make sure they had editing options. But Saira was magic. It was as if the rest of the world didn't exist when she got in character. Mia watched hungrily as Saira said her lines flawlessly. As much as she hated to admit it, the dialogue changes and the accent worked much better than what she'd originally approved. Saira had been right that it made the character more authentic. No, it wasn't just that—it made the character funnier, more tragic, more likable. The audiences would eat up Saira as Meera. Mia watched the director screens that showed the various camera angles. Saira wasn't the same old American sitcom star, nor was she like the South Asian actresses of previous shows; she brought her own brand of understated dramatization. It was the way she raised an eyebrow, or twitched her mouth, the way she moved her eyes and gave that look…. *that look.* Mia stood mesmerized. How could one woman be so beautiful?

Mia could scarcely believe how well things were going. By lunch time they were ahead of schedule.

Saira approached David, and they seemed to talk for quite a while. When both suddenly looked up in her direction, Mia scrambled, a little embarrassed that she was caught staring. David waved her over.

"Saira has an idea that we need to run past you."

Mia sighed.

"What is it now?"

"You seem so open to hearing my idea." Saira glared at her. Mia returned her stare with blazing eyes of her own.

"We're on a tight schedule," Mia said through clenched teeth.

"Hear her out," David interjected. Mia shot him a look. If anyone should be more stressed than she was about the taping schedule, it was him.

She folded her arms. "I'm listening."

Saira narrowed her eyes and placed her hands on her hips. "I was just saying that the next scene might work better in the kitchen than the living room."

"You want to change the location of the scene on the day we're taping it?" Mia said incredulously.

"It's the same set."

Mia looked at David. How was he not freaking out about this? It impacted him more than her. He had to move his camera crews, stage crews, and on and on.

"She's right that the scene might work better in the kitchen. Plus, she had a great idea about having the mother hold a spatula as she's talking with her hands with Meera trying to dodge the thing in addition to fighting off her mother's words."

"That's a whole change in scene, even for the Devi who's playing the mother. Plus you need to move all your cameras."

David shrugged. "There are two afternoon scenes in the kitchen so we can tape those along with this one after lunch. That will give me the lunch time to get the cameras situated."

Saira blew out a breath.

"If you two have it all figured out, then who am I to stand in the way."

She turned to leave when Saira's voice arrested her. "Can I talk to you. In private."

Saira's dressing room was the most convenient. It would take them fifteen minutes each way to walk to Mia's offices. Saira had her own trailer. Inside, the outfits of the day were hanging on a rack. A dresser, couch, and small table and chair were the only other furniture. Nothing sexy at all about the dressing room. No bed, and the couch looked uncomfortable as hell.

Mia followed behind Saira but stood by the door, one foot on the downward step. Saira took off her shoes, then began removing the pajamas that she'd been wearing for the morning scenes. Mia held up a hand. "What're you doing?"

Saira removed the pants and threw them on the couch. "I'm getting ready for the next scene. Aren't you the one that keeps reminding me what a tight schedule we're on?"

She tugged off her top and stood there in a lacy beige bra and panties that might as well not have been there. She reached behind her to take off the bra.

"Stop!" Mia hadn't mean to shout.

Saira raised a brow in that maddening way she did when she knew she'd made a point.

"I hope this is not about last night."

Once again Saira raised her brow. "I think you made it pretty clear that you didn't want more than a one-night stand."

Mia straightened. "That's right. So what do we have to talk about?"

"If you've forgotten, we are doing a show together. A show that's really important to me, and I'm tired of you rolling your eyes every time I bring up something."

"Saira, you have no idea how your little ideas create work for the rest of us. Because of your script changes, the writers were up past midnight, the camera crew and director had to be here an hour early to go over the timing changes. There are downstream repercussions that I have to worry about. Plus, there's the fact that you manipulated the network execs to get script approval into your contract ten seconds before filming was scheduled to begin. So excuse me if I don't jump for joy every time you have a bright idea."

Saira visibly flinched but Mia was not sorry for her harsh tone. Saira deserved it. She was used to everyone capitulating to her, and it was time Mia called Saira out on her manipulations.

Saira opened, then closed her mouth. She grabbed a robe off the hook and put it on. Not that it helped. Mia couldn't not notice her hard nipples or the way the lace caressed the curve of her breast.

She took a step toward Mia. "You know what your problem is?"

Here we go again. The speech about how she's grown-up and has the experience to know better than me.

Mia lifted her chin. "I'm surc you're about to tell me."

"Your problem is that that you hate the fact that you want me. That you love me. That you want nothing more right now than to rip off my underwear and throw me down on that table."

Mia's entire body went hot. She reached behind her and grabbed the railing leading down the steps. It would take less than five seconds for her to reach the door.

"You have quite the opinion of yourself. If I remember correctly, you're the one that gave me your hotel key."

"And you came. We had an amazing time, and then you left with some mutterings about closure. If it was just about getting your rocks off, why come?"

Mia took a breath. "What do you want from me, Saira? Come out and say it. If it's not sex, then what is it?"

"I want us to talk. Not like this, but to really talk about us. There's still something between us, and it's more than just sex. I want us to sit down and hash it out, to figure out what there is, and more importantly, what there could be."

She took a step closer, and Mia felt the railing bite into her back as she leaned against it.

"Why are you so afraid to talk about it?"

"Fine, let's talk about it. What're your plans? Tell me what's changed since Fiji. Are you ready to come out? Do you want to sit down and talk about when you're going to tell your family that you're not hetero. When are you moving to LA? Do you have a lawyer drawing up divorce papers with your husband?"

Saira's pressed her lips together.

"That's what I thought. How about you invite me to have a conversation when you have the answers to those questions."

Nine

Saira sank down on the couch as Mia exited, slamming the trailer door behind her. Why hadn't she just said what she'd wanted to. *I'm ready to give it all up. But only if I can have you, Mia. I'll give up my career, my life in Mumba., I'll face my family, I'll face the world. But only if you're beside me.*

Before last night, she'd wondered whether she had romanticized what she and Mia had. First love was blinding, and Saira wanted to make sure that the happiness she envisioned with Mia was real. Just because none of her other relationships had made her feel Mia's magic didn't mean that Mia was the answer.

But last night had proved that she hadn't imagined it all. Their connection was special and she wasn't ready to give up on them.

But Mia wasn't ready to forgive her. Saira had hoped that getting her into bed would melt her anger, make her see that they still had something, open her heart to exploring how they could make it work between them.

Her eyes stung as tears washed through her mascara and eyeliner. *What was I thinking?* She'd come to LA thinking she would focus on the show, make sure it was a success, and then, when she was sure she could make it work, she'd rekindle things with Mia. Instead, she hadn't been able to keep her hands off Mia. She'd jumped the gun thinking that if they fell back in love, Saira would find the strength to do what she needed. But Mia wasn't going to solve her problems.

She called Rahul and told him what had happened.

"Babe, I'm sorry. Maybe you're focusing on the wrong thing."

"What do you mean?"

"You're trying to convince Mia that there's still something between you two. But your decisions can't revolve around Mia. You came to LA to see if you can build a new life. A life where you can live in the open, be in a real relationship. That was your goal before Mia became this show's producer."

Saira sniffed.

Rahul continued. "If Mia rejects you, which she has, by the way, are you changing your plans?

She shook her head, then realized Rahul wasn't on video. "No, I still want to try and make it in LA. I'm tired of doing background checks on women I meet and making them sign nondisclosure agreements on our first date. I'm tired of being alone."

"Gee, thanks."

"You know what I mean."

He sighed. "I do."

She stood. Rahul was right. She'd lost sight of her objective. She couldn't get her life back on track until she made sure *Life with Meera* was a success. It was time for her to stop playing nice—her career depended on it.

As the actors took their places, Mia stiffened. Saira was dressed in the saree that costume had designed for her, but the underlying blouse that she'd taken issue with was different. Mia had expressly declined the request for a new blouse. Had Saira gone behind her back again?

She walked up to her and tapped her on the shoulder. Saira threw her luscious hair back. The same hair that had fallen on Mia's chest yesterday. The same hair she had woven her fingers through as Saira's mouth licked and sucked and drove her mad.

"Where did that blouse come from?"

"It's mine."

"Excuse me?"

"I told you the old blouse didn't work. You wouldn't authorize a new one, so I decided to use one of my own."

"Without checking with me? We have to consider lighting and...."

"Lighting gets adjusted after all the actors are in place. I don't understand why you're making such a big deal. I'm using one of my existing blouses. It's better stitching and fit anyway, and it looks better with the saree." She stepped back and spread her arms.

Why did she always look so good? Mia

hated to admit it but the blouse was much nicer. It was a modern cut with a sweetheart neckline. Saira's waist and cleavage was on full display. The saree was wrapped perfectly to show off all her curves.

"The point is not that the blouse is bad, the point is that you can't just change wardrobe. Does this work in India? Do they let you waltz onto the set with whatever you want to wear?"

"First, they know how to dress me in Mumbai. Second, they would've stitched the new blouse. Now if there's nothing else, I believe they're ready for the shot."

What!

Saira turned away from her. No, she didn't just turn away, she dismissed her. What had happened? Just an hour ago Saira was begging for her attention, trying to talk to her, seduce her. Now it was as if Mia was an annoyance Saira didn't want to deal with.

Mia strode over to David, who was staring intently at the bank of screens in front of him. "Did you really allow Saira to waltz onto the set wearing her own clothes?"

David didn't bother looking up. "It's one piece of the costume. What's the big deal?"

Mia blew out a breath. "The big deal is that Saira is walking all over you. Yesterday she was asking for wholesale script changes, and when I wouldn't give them to her, she made a deal with the network. Today it's costume changes. We're running a show here, David. we can't let the talent…."

David held up a hand, then turned to her. "I once had to send an intern clear across town at five in the morning so my star actor could have a particular muffin from a specific bakery. Then there was the prima donna who screamed at the makeup artists because they couldn't magically make her wrinkles disappear." He looked back onto the screens. Saira was in the picture, adjusting her saree. Mia couldn't help but notice the way that blouse dipped low on her back, exposing that piece of skin that drove Saira delirious with desire when Mia kissed it. "In the grand scheme of actor issues, Saira's are not worth our time. Her script changes are actually good—she's not trying to get more airtime. And you know as well as I do that we've got an all-white writers' room, so it's good to have someone make sure we aren't doing something that will piss off a whole bunch of South Asians."

"Sunil is also part of the writing team."

"Glad to know we have the token Indian who was born and raised in SoCal and has to call his parents to translate any Hindi words we want in the script."

Mia wanted to rage at him, but the wind was suddenly out of her sails. David was right. She'd had the same concerns when she had first taken over the show. So much so that she'd gotten a sensitivity read on the script.

She dropped into a chair. Saira was getting to her. Mia's every decision since Saira had arrived had been based on an emotional reaction. She hadn't been thinking clearly. Once again Saira had swept Mia up in her vortex of chaos—and Mia had allowed herself to get swept up. She had slept with the star of her show! If word got out, Mia would be ruined. Not because set relationships didn't happen, but because she and Saira had been at odds, and any conflict between them would be perceived as personal rather than professional. Mia didn't need that for her first big show. *God, how clichéd—producer gets her first big break and she throws it all away for hot sex.* Producers were more easily replaced than stars.

"Mia!"

She looked up to see Gail standing with her hands on her hips. "What is wrong with you? I've been texting you for the last hour. I had to run down here to find you."

Mia looked at the phone in her hand. She had it on silent for the taping, but she usually checked her messages every few minutes. On a show like this, there was always a crisis brewing somewhere, whether it was equipment malfunction, an unexpected budget spend, or a hissy fit from a writer, actor, director. It was endless.

She stood. David was getting ready to start shooting, so Gail pulled her outside the studio doors. "They want to see you on the thirty-fourth floor."

That can't be good.

"What's going on?"

"I talked to Chris's assistant but she was zipped tight."

What had Saira pulled now?

Taking a breath, she made her way to the studio offices. Apparently, they wanted her to sit in the waiting room until the network kings had a second to spare for her between meetings. She waited for over an hour, texting Gail to find out how taping was going. Apparently, it was going even better than it had in the morning. They were staying ahead of schedule.

When Chris was finally ready, Mia had reached a new level of impatience. Her email was overflowing with a million little things, and she still had to do the daily wrap and go through the checklist for tomorrow. Plus, she had to go to the bathroom, but there was no way she was going to risk missing her chance—they'd probably make her wait until yet another meeting was over.

As she walked into the room, she noticed there were a number of other people there whose faces she recognized from the portraits hanging in the lobby and hallway. Half the network executives were there. They weren't sitting on the couch drinking whiskey but were seated around the small conference room table.

Chris motioned her toward an empty chair that an assistant pulled up to the table.

"We don't have a lot of time so I'm going to just say it. We're canceling *Life with Meera*."

Shit. Had they found out about her and Saira? She shook the thought from her head. That would be a reason to fire her, not cancel the show.

She swallowed. "Why?"

"Not enough of the streaming services have picked it up for us to be profitable."

"Filming has begun. You'll have to pay out most of the actors. We've essentially already spent over 60 percent of the budget."

"A loss we can take. We still have to consider the remaining budget, plus marketing expenses. And with Saira renegotiating her contract, more of the budget is free."

Mia felt an unexpected anger roil deep in her belly. They had taken advantage of Saira. All along she'd thought Saira had offered up a fee reduction for script approval, but now she strongly suspected that slimy

Chris had talked her into it, knowing full well they'd be canceling the show.

"We've also recently acquired the rights to a tell-all for one of the European royals, so we need to free up some cash to get that made. It's going to take the slot we had for *Life with Meera*."

Mia took a breath. She could argue, list all the reasons why the show was better than yet another royal documentary, brainstorm ways in which she could save money, even come up with marketing ideas. But one look around the table and she knew what this was about. Someone was cashing in a chit with someone else and *Life with Meera* was going to pay the price. Mia was going to pay the price, along with Saira and David and all the other actors and crew. These network weenies didn't care.

"What if I can find a way to get the streaming services interested?"

"And how would you do that?" The question came from a silver-haired man in a really nice Brioni suit.

Mia held up a finger, then pulled out her phone. With a few clicks, she pulled up

Rahul Chandan's Instagram page then held up the phone. Seeing the squinting eyes, she handed the phone to Chris, who took a look and passed it around.

"Saira's husband is an international star. That one post from his Instagram account has more than a million likes. His fans posted additional photos that have hundreds of thousands. He has star power. Now imagine a few more posts like this with the hashtag *Life with Meera*. It'll create buzz."

The silver-haired man peered at the picture. "I know this guy. One of the other studios is courting him for a major movie."

Mia waited. She'd learned the hard way that in a room full of men, she needed to let them come up with the obvious plan so they thought it was their idea. Networks still worked on the GOBSAT principle. Good Old Boys Sitting Around a Table.

"Can you get him to do a cameo, do some show promos? For free?"

Sure, and while I'm at it, why don't I ask Santa Claus for another million dollars and two months so I can do the show properly.

"I'll talk to Saira."

"Report back tomorrow morning. We need to move fast on this."

Sure. I've been busting my ass for the last two months working eighteen-hour days to get everything ready, but you only have a few seconds to consider whether or not to throw the whole thing out.

"I doubt Rahul can make this decision without consulting his lawyer, publicist and agent. You can't expect an answer overnight. Plus, India is 10.5 hours ahead in time."

"Good, then it's early in the day there. Find a way to make it work."

Yes your majesty.

She gave a curt nod and left before she felt the urge to say something that could get her fired from the network, not just the show.

Back in the studio, filming was wrapping up for the day. They had made good progress. Mia gestured for Gail and directed her to ask Saira to come to her office once she was free. She debated telling David, then decided against it. Mia wanted David focused on filming. David was only on this show because Peter had recruited him. Someone of his talent would get scooped up in a second.

If he thought the show was going to get canceled, he might bail, and Mia couldn't afford that. She crossed her fingers he wouldn't hear about it from someone else. She avoided telling Gail as well. As much as she loved her friend, Gail could be a bit of a gossip, and Mia couldn't risk this getting out.

By the time Mia got to her office, she was exhausted and her to-do list had gotten longer. She got through the smaller items, then began tackling the budget reports. She and David were scheduled to meet later in the evening to go over the dailies. He was a night owl and liked to take a break after filming. It would be another late night for her, and not quite as satisfying as last night.

Mia looked at her watch. *Why isn't Saira here yet?* She texted Gail, who replied Saira had left an hour ago. Sighing, Mia texted Saira. Why was everything so difficult with her? Maybe she shouldn't talk to her about getting Rahul to endorse the show. Maybe the show getting canceled was a good thing. Saira would go back to her fabulous Bollywood life, and Mia could move on. She'd find another show, another series, maybe she'd branch out and do a movie.

When an hour went by without Saira texting her back, Mia called her. *Voice mail.*

She's ignoring me.

Mia didn't bother leaving a message. She called the hotel and asked for Saira's room. The phone rang for a good minute before a breathless Saira answered the phone.

Mia hung up without saying anything. She grabbed her purse and headed to the hotel.

Ten

Saira was more mentally exhausted than physically. She'd enjoyed her first day of filming. Her fellow actors were thoroughly professional, and David was eccentric but clearly good at his job. But she'd spent the whole day either trying to avoid Mia or find her. Despite her promise to Rahul, Saira couldn't pretend that Mia didn't exist. Or forget what had happened between them last night. When Mia asked to meet with her, Saira decided to ignore the request. She had no desire to be alone with Mia. Rahul was right—Saira had to focus on her career, on this show. Her Hollywood agent had called her before she hopped into the shower. He'd gotten her email about finding her something better, and he'd beaten the bushes, even suggested Saira read for parts, but there was nothing. Saira was not as well-known as Rahul or Priyanka Chopra. Not in America. She was still a nobody as far as Hollywood was concerned.

Rahul would help if she asked. He had contacts, and his agent had a wider reach than her own. But she'd made a promise to herself that she wouldn't exploit their relationship. Rahul wasn't just her husband, he was her best friend, and she knew he'd do anything for her. He had been taken advantage of earlier in his life by his parents and then a childhood sweetheart, both of whom ended up wanting nothing more than money from him. He viewed every relationship with a large measure of suspicion. Saira had asked for his help in getting Mia the producer's role. She had agonized over that decision. Rahul had done it for her, but the request hadn't felt right. And what had that favor resulted in? She'd wanted Mia as the producer thinking that Mia would understand the problems with the script and work with Saira to fix them. Instead, Mia was fighting her every step of the way.

Who was she kidding? Saira had seen the producer role as a way to get close to Mia again. All that had accomplished was an hour of pure pleasure that left Saira even more wanting than she had been. When Gail asked her to go meet with Mia in her office, Saira purposely ignored the request. She didn't want to be alone with Mia, didn't want to smell her, look at her, touch her. She had enough problems; she didn't need additional reminders that she was in love with a woman who wouldn't love her back.

She sighed and picked up the room service menu. She wasn't particularly hungry but she had to eat and get to bed. The makeup artist had had to put hemorrhoid cream under her eyes today to reduce the puffiness. She hadn't slept last night, tossing and turning and going over every second with Mia in her mind, feeling her touch on Saira's skin, remembering the way she'd tasted when Saira licked and sucked her, smelling the scent of Mia on her mouth and fingers. *Damn her!*

Saira ordered a Cobb salad, decaf coffee and chocolate mousse cake. After the day she'd had, she deserved a treat. She was tempted to add wine to her order, then remembered it kept her up at night. She was getting to an age when the lack of sleep showed on her face. She needed to look fabulous for this show. Flawless and beautiful, the classic Indian beauty to win the American audience. She didn't have Priyanka's lips or Rahul's charm, but she had naturally luminous skin that was the envy of her fellow actresses.

Her hair still wet from the shower, she rubbed in an Ayurvedic hair oil, then left it to air-dry while she slept. Binita, her hairdresser at home, had done wonders for her hair in the last few years by shifting Saira from chemical products to natural oils and reducing the use of hair dryers that damaged the roots and structure. She completed her skin care routine with all natural Ayurvedic creams and settled into bed to wait for room service.

At the sound of the door knock, she looked

at her watch. *Boy, they are fast.* She belted her robe firmly and padded across the suite.

She opened the door and stopped short. “Mia! What are you doing here.”

“I asked to meet with you.”

“I was busy. You can’t come barging into my hotel. How did you even get up here?” The elevators need a key card to get to the room floors.

Mia held up a white card. “Forgot to give this back to you yesterday.”

Saira snatched the card and made to close the door. She could not have Mia in her hotel room. Not with her completely naked under the bathrobe, her body already itching for Mia’s touch.

Mia held out her arm. “Please, this is not about us. It’s about the show. I need your help.”

This is new.

Saira waved her in. The suite had a small living area with a dining table and four chairs, a couch and TV. The bedroom was only a few steps away. When Saira did location shoots for her Bollywood movies, she got an entire apartment with multiple rooms, plus quarters for her maid. When she had FaceTimed her agent in Mumbai, he had been aghast at the "third class" place they had put her up in. But Saira knew how to pick her battles, and the hotel room was not the sword to die on.

She sat at the dining table. Best to have something solid between her and Mia.

"Please keep what I'm about to tell you between us."

Mia frowned but nodded.

"The network wants to cancel *Life with Meera*."

The words bottomed out Saira's stomach. She was counting on the show to launch her career. Her agent had pretty much told her that she needed to wait until the show released and hope it was a success if she wanted the type of offers in Hollywood that she got from Mumbai.

"What do they want?"

It didn't matter if they were network executives in LA or money laundering film producers in Mumbai, they all threatened cancellations when they were looking to get something for free.

"They want Rahul to make a cameo appearance and do some show promotions." Mia gulped, as if embarrassed to say the next part.

"And they want him to do it for free."

Mia nodded. Saira shook her head in disgust. "The industry is the same around the world." She looked Mia squarely in the eyes. "Tell them no."

Mia jolted. "What do you mean tell them no? They'll cancel the show. Can't you ask Rahul whether he'd be willing at least?"

Saira shook her head. "I will not take advantage of Rahul. And these network people are bluffing you. They want to force you and me to give them something for free. When you refuse, they'll shrug their shoulders and move on."

Mia took a breath. "Look, things might work that way in Bollywood, but shows get canceled here all the time. I don't think they're bluffing. That's probably why they so easily gave you script approval in exchange for cutting your fee. You are the most expensive actor we have on the show."

She shook her head. "Did you read my revised contract? It says that if they cancel the show or fail to air all ten episodes for any reason, then they owe me my original fee."

Mia must have missed that. She raised a brow. "That was smart."

Saira crossed her arms. "I know what I'm doing. If you think you've got snakes here in your management, I've got snake charmers in Mumbai who are so good at manipulation that you dance to their *been*—" she mimed the flute that snake charmers used "—without even knowing it."

Mia smiled and Saira's heart caught like a string on a guitar pick. Saira loved how natural Mia was. She didn't lotion and potion her face until it shone, didn't scrub and plump her lips, tweeze and thread her brows. She had that natural beauty that was effortless. Ten years had put some lines on her face, taken away some of the fat that used to be on her cheeks and given her smile and eyes a more reserved, tentative quality. Yet she was even more breathtaking than she had been in Fiji. The way Mia's hazel eyes crinkled when she smiled shot daggers through Saira's heart. W*hy? Why am I so attracted* *to her? There are so many beautiful women in this world. Why can't they make me feel like she does?*

"They know Rahul is in town. He's created some social media stir passionately kissing his wife in our studio lobby."

Jealous, are we?

"I told you, our marriage is not real. It's based on friendship. He knows I'm a lesbian."

"Is that what you are now? I thought you were bi, or fluid."

Saira tilted her head. "I didn't have a supportive family and culture to help me figure out what I am. Took me a little longer than you. Give me a break."

Mia bit her lip and Saira shifted in her seat. "Why can't you ask Rahul? Even if the execs are bluffing, which for the record I don't think they are, their idea is a good one. Having a cameo from Rahul and publicity might help get interest from the streaming services. That'll be good for our show."

"First of all, wouldn't a cameo change the script, costumes, lighting, and what were the other things—" she clicked her fingers

"—camera timings etc. etc. Those changes take time and effort and we're already on a tight schedule."

Mia's cheeks reddened and Saira felt a jolt of heat through her. Mia's cheeks also colored like that when she was aroused.

"Look, I want to apologize to you. I haven't been fair in listening to your suggestions. I admit that you've been right about some things."

"Some things?"

"Seeing you again threw me off. I haven't been myself."

Saira leaned forward. "Seeing you threw me off too."

It wouldn't take much to lean over just a bit more and kiss her. From there it wouldn't be much to pull her into the bedroom.

"Do you know why it's important for me that we get this show right? That we don't perpetuate cultural stereotypes?" It was a rhetorical question. The only people who knew what had happened with Kayra were her family and Rahul. Mia knew about her sister's condition but not how she'd become that way.

Mia frowned. *That's right. You never thought to ask me.* Saira was tired of fighting with Mia on every little thing. It was only day one of filming. There were still twelve weeks to go. It was time Mia knew.

"Kayra was only fifteen when I asked her to do this show called *Ram ki Maya*. They had offered it to me but I wanted a break. I was tired of being responsible for paying the family bills. I thought if I got Kayra into the industry, it would ease the burden on me."

Mia reached out and placed a hand on top of hers.

"I didn't really take the time to look at the script or follow along as filming progressed. Turned out that the show was a satire on the classic Ramayana. But it went too far. When it aired, there was a public outcry that the show had desecrated a sacred text. Kayra's role was Seeta, who we call Seeta *maiya*, mother Seeta. The show questioned a really key principle about whether Seeta was still pure after being held captive by Ravana—the evil demon who kidnapped her. The show made light of this assumption, implying that Seeta had an affair with Ravana.

It was in really bad humor and enraged a lot of people. The show went too far."

Saira swallowed against the lump in her throat. "The public wasn't just mad, they went fanatical. There were protests and burning of posters depicting the show, it was bad. They took their anger out on Kayra. We got her bodyguards because of all the threats against her. But they couldn't protect her from a particularly brutal crowd…." Her mouth soured as she thought about the image of Kayra after that attack. "A whole group of people descended on her, kicking and beating her with shoes and sticks. She was in such bad shape." Her voice cracked. "Took multiple surgeries and physical therapy."

Mia squeezed her hand. "Oh, Saira, I'm so sorry. Why didn't you tell me before?"

"It is not something I talk about." The truth was that she'd never wanted to tell Mia. Never wanted to see the disappointment Saira saw in her mother's eyes every time Kayra's name came up. *Kayra is not as strong as you. This wouldn't have happened to you.* There wasn't a day that went by when Saira didn't wish that she hadn't given that role to Kayra. She had ruined her sister's life. Kayra had healed from her physical injuries but never really recovered mentally. The center in Switzerland had been great for her anxiety.

"After what happened to Kayra, I don't just accept a script. It's my name and face out there. When the public sees something they don't like, they don't blame the producer, the director, the writers or even the studio. They blame the actor. They direct their anger, and their hatred, at the person on the screen."

"Oh, Saira, I wish I'd known. I can't believe you've been dealing with this all by yourself."

How did she tell Mia that Saira was too embarrassed. Too ashamed. Mia's hand was still on top of hers and she turned her palm and laced her fingers with Mia's. "I didn't want you to know. Fiji was an escape for me. It was the first time I was myself, the first time I'd let myself forget all my responsibilities, all my guilt."

"Guilt? Why do you feel guilty?"

"That role was mine. If I hadn't given it to Kayra just so I could sleep later in the mornings and have more free time to read books, her life wouldn't have been ruined."

Mia stood and came to kneel beside Saira. "No, no Saira. You can't blame yourself for what happened to Kayra. That is not your fault. If there is anyone to blame here, frankly, it's your parents. You were a child yourself, and you needed a break. That didn't mean that your sister had to pick up the mantle…."

"I was twenty. Hardly a child. Kayra was the child, and I am her big sister."

Mia stood and enveloped her in a hug, Saira's head resting on her belly and chest. She breathed in deeply, tears streaming down her face. After it had happened, her parents had been shattered, and it had been up to Saira to figure out how to fix it all. To get Kayra the medical attention she needed and then the ongoing rehabilitation. It had all fallen to Saira to organize and pay for.

"I am so tired, Mia. I am so, so tired. Tired of acting, tired of the responsibility, of the burden of it all."

Mia held her tight. "It's a lot for anyone to take on."

"I left you in Fiji because my parents showed up, and they reminded me of the responsibilities I had. It wasn't just about having the courage to come out to my parents. I couldn't jeopardize my career. Kayra was healing physically but she was a mess mentally. The facilities in India aren't that great, so we sent her to Europe and eventually Switzerland. All that costs money. My career isn't just supporting designer handbags…."

"Oh, Saira. Why didn't you just tell me all this. Why pretend that what we had was meaningless."

"Because I know you. If I'd told you what I'm telling you now, you would've lectured me on how Kayra isn't my responsibility and somehow convinced me to prioritize myself."

"You're right. That's exactly what I would've done. No offense, but your parents are taking advantage of you. Kayra is their responsibility. They are the ones who let her take your role because they wanted another cash cow."

Saira stiffened. She'd been afraid of this. Mia didn't share her cultural values. She didn't understand that it was the children's responsibility to take care of their parents.

"See, this is why I didn't want to tell you. You don't understand. Our culture is different. We take care of family, even if it means sacrificing ourselves. Kayra is my responsibility. She is my sister. Even if I weren't responsible for her condition…"

"You are not responsible for what happened to her…."

"She is my sister, and I need to take care of her as long as I'm physically capable."

Mia took a deep breath and Saira leaned back, pushing herself out of Mia's arms.

"I thought it would be cleaner if we just broke up. I didn't want to spend my life wondering what could have been. Remember I wasn't as big a star as I am now. Hollywood wasn't as much of an option. And we were young…"

"I've spent all this time being angry at you…"

Saira sighed. "I know. I thought you'd forget about me, and I about you. But honestly, what we have together…"

Mia nodded. Saira could see it in her eyes. She still cared about her. Still loved her. Saira felt lighter.

"I'm tired. Do you mind if I go to bed?"

Mia nodded but stood there. Saira called room service and canceled her order. The little bit of appetite she'd had was gone. She was exhausted.

"Can I stay with you tonight? Sleep with you? Just sleep?"

Saira raised her brows, then nodded in relief. She needed Mia. She offered Mia some of her pajamas and crawled into bed in her robe. She turned to her side and Mia spooned her, hugging her tightly.

Saira couldn't help the tears that streamed down her face. Years of stress, shame, anxiety, frustration and loneliness poured out of her. Mia just held her, occasionally sitting up to wipe her tears, sometimes with her bare hands, other times with the sleeve of her pajama top. They didn't talk. Saira was totally spent. Mia held on to her, occasionally rubbing her back.

Saira fell asleep eventually and slept better than she had in years. When she woke, she turned over in her bed and found it empty.

Mia was gone.

Eleven

Mia hated sneaking out of Saira's room early in the morning, but she didn't want to wake her. Saira had had a rough night and she needed to rest. She had debated writing a note but hadn't known what to say. She would see Saira soon enough, and she still didn't know what to say.

All this time, Mia had assumed Saira didn't want to lose her lifestyle and idol status. The truth was so much more heartbreaking. *I wish she'd told me in Fiji.* They would've worked something out. Mia would've helped Saira figure out what to do, could have been there for her, helped and supported her. Even as she'd held Saira last night, Mia had ached for her, the pain she had endured, the constant stress she was under.

Good or bad, she had several fires to keep her mind occupied. David was mad that she'd blown off the review of dailies with him. She still had to report to Chris, and if he decided to move forward with canceling the show, she'd have to break the news to the crew. She'd have to tell Saira.

She had asked the front desk to wake Saira an hour before her reporting time. The hotel was only fifteen minutes from the studio; that should've given Saira enough time to get there. Makeup and hair would be in the studio, so all Saira had to do was shower, throw on a pair of jeans and sunglasses and grab a tea. Saira didn't eat breakfast.

When she hadn't shown up fifteen minutes past her call time, Mia began to pace. She texted, called, then dispatched an intern to her room. She should've woken Saira and said goodbye, made sure she was okay.

Thirty minutes past call time, Saira finally stormed in. Her hair was pulled back into a severe ponytail, her face devoid of makeup. She'd thrown on a T-shirt and jeans that curved around her in just the right ways. She searched the room then made a beeline for Mia.

Uh-oh. Should've left a note.

Mia held up her hands as Saira approached, her quick walk and blazing eyes clearly conveying her anger. "Sorry I left the way I did, I didn't want to…"

"Did you call Rahul and ask him to do cameo and free promo for this show?" Saira was yelling and everyone was starting to stare.

Mia grabbed her arm. "Can we talk outside?"

Saira shook her off. "No thank you, we can talk here. Did you call Rahul?"

"You didn't want to ask him, so I did. As the producer of the show."

"On my behalf."

"I made no such representations."

"C'mon Mia." She gave her a pointed look and Mia shifted on her feet. She had called Rahul after Saira fell asleep the night before. He had been surprised to hear from her but clearly knew all about her and Saira.

He'd asked Mia to stay the night to make sure Saira would be okay. When Mia had explained the situation, he had readily said yes. She'd known Saira would be upset but it had to be done.

"Rahul was happy to do it."

"Rahul isn't the one who has a problem with this—I do."

"Why? I get not wanting to ask your husband for a favor but you didn't. I did."

"He did it for me."

"As he should. You've done plenty for him."

Mia gave Saira a pointed look. She'd asked Rahul whether it bothered him that Mia was spending the night. That's when he'd told her that he was gay. Rahul also confessed that he had been the one who had inadvertently ended their relationship in Fiji. When Saira called him from Fiji, he'd been going through an identity crisis of his own. He had just been blackmailed by his first sexual partner and projected his fears onto Saira when he saw the Facebook posts of her and Mia. He had mistakenly gone to her parents, thinking he was protecting her.

After the conversation with Rahul, Mia felt even more like a shit for being angry with Saira. She had been nothing but a good daughter, sister and friend, had given up her own happiness for everyone else she cared about.

"He's my husband. That was my call to make."

All eyes were on them. This was not the time to have this discussion. "I am the show's producer and I am well within my rights to ask another star to make a cameo appearance."

Saira opened her mouth, then closed it. She turned on her heels and marched to her makeup seat. She waved her hands dismissively at the gawkers. Chris had given them two weeks to see if Rahul's social media buzz would create interest from the streaming services. The world of TV had changed since Mia had been an intern. Back then, it was all about advertisers and making sure the network affiliates would pick up the show. Now shows were sold not just to the network affiliates who aired it live, but to the streaming services, some of which got the show shortly after it aired, and others got it later. The amount they paid determined when they got the show, and the more demand there was for a show, the higher its purchase price. Rahul had already posted on Instagram announcing his cameo on #LifeWithMeera. It was approaching several hundred thousand likes just an hour after posting.

Mia sighed. She would have to set things right with Saira at the lunch break. Mia had newfound admiration for her. The woman had more responsibilities than anyone she knew. Mia felt stressed about paying her rent and the payment on her car, especially when she was between projects. She couldn't imagine what it was like for Saira, having to support her whole family, including medical expenses for her sister.

Mia made herself scarce once shooting started. Now that some of the kinks had been worked out and the actors had gotten a feel for each other, shooting was going well. During a break, David approached her. "Why didn't you tell me the network was thinking of canceling the show?" He was whispering, but Mia shot him a look and pulled him into a corner, keeping an eye for eavesdroppers. "Look, I just found out yesterday and I didn't want to panic everyone until it was a done deal. Sounds like the network is having trouble selling the show to the streaming services but I got Saira's husband to do a cameo and some promos."

"Yes, thank you for telling me about that as well. He's only available tomorrow so we have to get the script, costumes..."

Mia held up a hand. "I already talked to the writers' room. We're going to integrate him into the café scene we're already filming. Costume is going to use something they already have in Rahul's size, and I'll schedule a meeting with the entire crew after we wrap up tonight so we are ready."

David crossed his arms. "You seem to have thought of everything."

"It all happened so fast. I'm sorry I didn't consult you, but you know that none of this can happen without you."

"You forget I exist sometimes."

"Of course not! You know this show was over budget. I only did it because you were the director." She gave him an appeasing smile. Stroking egos was the most hated part of her job, but one that she had become very talented at.

Gail was the next one to corner her. She had heard the news from David's assistant, who had overheard him muttering to himself after *he* heard the news from an intern in Chris's office. Gail strongly suspected that David was sleeping with that intern, who was thankfully in her twenties but at least thirty years younger than David.

Mia sighed. She'd have to address the potential cancellation with the crew in the evening. By then, even the night cleaning crew would know that the show was on the chopping block.

During lunch, Saira walked off to her dressing room. Mia assembled a plate of food from the catering table and made her way to the trailer. She knocked several times before Saira finally opened the door. She was dressed in a long silk robe that hugged her body way too tightly. She looked at Mia with narrowed eyes, then stepped inside, letting her enter. The dressing room was a mess with clothes strewn everywhere, empty bottles of water here and there, and wilting flowers that hadn't been put in a vase. Mia made a mental note to send an assistant in to clean. Saira wasn't used to keeping herself organized.

Mia pushed some clothes off the coffee table and put the plate down. "I got you some quinoa salad and a falafel sandwich."

Saira eyed the plate. "And the mini crème brûlée is for you?"

Mia smiled. "I'd be willing to share if you let me explain."

Saira sat on the little dressing room stool, grabbed the sandwich and took a bite. As Mia suspected, she hadn't had any breakfast. "You shouldn't have gone to Rahul behind my back."

"I'm sorry. Chris gave me until this morning to confirm Rahul. You were in no shape for us to argue about this. I should've waited and woken you up early this morning, but to tell you the truth, I wanted an excuse to talk to Rahul alone." She gave her a small smile.

"You still think I'm sleeping with Rahul?"

"No!" Mia reached out and grabbed

Saira's hand. She struggled to find the right words to explain her sudden urge to talk to Rahul, knowing how intertwined he was in Saira's life. It was a ridiculous idea, but Mia couldn't help feeling that she needed to connect with him; there was a missing piece to the puzzle of Saira's life, and Rahul was it. "You've been with him for ten years, known him since you were a child," Mia said, her voice tinged with a hint of envy. "I can't help feeling a little jealous of the time he's had with you. I wanted to know what he was like. I don't know, I thought it would bring me closer to you."

Saira looked down, then leaned over and gave her a quick kiss on the forehead. "Rahul was a child star like me. Except he has a very different relationship with his parents than I do. They were very exploitative, and Rahul had to hire a lawyer when he was fifteen to get independence."

"He filed for emancipation?"

"Yes, except there is no such thing in India. Children are considered property and there are no laws protecting children from the financial exploitation of their parents. His case went nowhere."

Why didn't you file for emancipation with Rahul? Mia wisely kept her mouth shut. If there was one thing that had been clear last night, it was that Saira believed it was her responsibility to take care of her parents and sister. She didn't feel taken advantage of.

"Finally at the age of eighteen, he had to give up all of the money he made as a child, including ongoing royalties for old films, and start new." Saira took another bite of her sandwich, and Mia handed her a bottle of water to wash it down. "It didn't end there. His parents sued him for ongoing support. That went on for like ten years, and they were going to lose but then they blackmailed him."

Mia's heart lurched as it suddenly became clear. "Rahul told me he's gay. His parents used that against him, didn't they?"

Saira stared at her. "He told you?"

When Mia nodded, she raised her brows. "You must've had a really good conversation. That's not something he shares. His parents threatened to out him and ruin his career. So he pays them hush money. It's supposed to be a monthly sum but it never ends. Every few months they have an urgent cash need. You know, his mother sees a diamond necklace she must have, or his father wants to buy the new MG SUV."

"That must be awful for him."

"I try to be the one person in his life that isn't exploiting him, that isn't always asking for things. I already asked him for help getting this role, and then getting you as producer...."

You don't want to treat him the way your parents treat you. Mia almost said the words out loud but managed to restrain herself.

"I'm sorry I went behind your back. But, if it makes you feel any better, Rahul was happy to do it."

"He also hands over the checks to his parents with a smile and some dialogue about how it's important to have a parent's blessing and good wishes for a successful life."

Mia slumped into the couch, not bothering to move the saree that was underneath her. Saira stood and pulled her off the couch. "Don't sit there, you'll crush the saree. As it is, your costume people did a horrible job of pressing it."

"Pressing it?"

Saira rolled her eyes. "Ironing."

Mia stood and helped Saira redrape the saree on the couch. "Shit, this is for today?"

Saira nodded. "That's why I was late this morning. They delivered this to me and it had so many wrinkles, I had to get them to send me an iron and board."

"You ironed this?"

"You think I don't know how to iron?"

"Honestly, no. Have you ever ironed before?"

Saira smiled. "Actually no. I had to video call my assistant in India. It was like the middle of the night there. She talked me through it."

They both laughed.

"You know what, you shouldn't have to be figuring out how to iron a saree. I'll talk to costume about getting someone who knows Indian clothes."

"Thank you! I had to tie the saree myself yesterday."

"Why didn't you say something?"

Saira raised her brow. "And have you bite off my head? I've been picking my battles."

Mia sighed. "You're right. I've been so wound up about you, about us, that I haven't been really listening to you about the changes to the show."

Saira picked up the mini crème brûlée. "You can make it up to me by letting me eat this whole thing."

Mia grabbed a fork and popped a small bite in her mouth. "Not a chance. You know how I feel about sharing dessert."

Saira set down the small ramekin after gobbling the rest of the crème brûlée in three bites. "As I recall, you are perfectly willing to share your dessert, as long as I'm licking it off your body." She pulled Mia by the shirt and kissed her. Mia expected the kiss to be hard, but it was gentle, maddeningly so. Saira cupped her cheek and touched her lips to Mia's, gently kissing, tugging and tasting her. Their breasts brushed against each other, and Mia placed her hand on Saira's waist to tug her closer. She moved her hand to Saira's hips, longing to touch her through the silky robe, but Saira pulled back.

Mia's body was hot, her core wet. She needed Saira. She wanted Saira, naked and lying on that couch.

"If you're worried about the saree, I'll reiron it."

Saira smiled. "I don't want it to be like last time between us. Quick and dirty, as you Americans say." She touched Mia's cheek. "If you're ready to be with me, come spend the night. We can order room service, stay up late, wake up slowly in the morning. Tomorrow's not a workday."

It wasn't a workday for Saira—Sunday wasn't a shooting day—but Mia still had things she needed to do.

"On one condition."

Saira raised an eyebrow and Mia took a breath to try and cool her body. The idea of a night with Saira was enough to send her pulsing with need. "Wait up for me."

Twelve

Rahul showed up for his cameo appearance with his usual swagger, dressed in jeans and a deceptively bedraggled T-shirt. Apparently, he had a fan base among the crew. They were all used to dealing with stars, so were reserved in asking for selfies, but the excitement was infectious. Saira remembered a time when people just asked for autographs; now she had to look selfie perfect everywhere she went.

She sneaked a look at Mia, who was standing back. They'd spent the night together, talking, making love, then talking some more. It was different than it had been in Fiji.

There was more raw honesty between them. Mia had told her all about how hard it had been for her as a female producer in a male dominated industry, how she still wished for a reconciliation with her parents, even though they still didn't accept her sexuality. She'd never seen Mia so vulnerable and it made her feel even closer to her. Mia had opened up about how hurt she'd been when her parents kicked her out of the house, how she'd missed their presence in her life all these years. Saira better understood why she was so insistent on living her life openly. Mia had given up everything she valued, her home and the love she shared with her mother, so she didn't feel the crushing vice of her secret every day. It inspired Saira, made her want the same for hcrself, and for Rahul. While he was smiling for his fans now, he'd been stressed all morning. The story with Hosiang was catching steam on social media. They both lived in fear that a picture, an overhead comment could ruin their lives in a hot minute. It was no way to live, and she was done with it.

Saira introduced Rahul to Mia. They

hugged as if they were old friends, and Saira felt a rush of warmth and irritation. “Now, now, you two better not be scheming behind my back.” She’d meant to sound teasing, but the words came out accusatory.

Rahul kissed her on the cheek. “We are absolutely scheming. Somebody has to take care of you, and now I have a partner in crime.”

“I understand you have a party to get to, so I’ll see you both tomorrow.” Mia raised her hand to wave goodbye but Rahul touched her shoulder.

“Why don’t you come with us?”

Saira raised a brow. “Isn’t it invitation only?” Her own agent had called her twice this morning to make sure she could go to this exclusive party with Rahul. She needed the exposure.

Rahul shrugged. “I’m invited. I don’t think they’ll mind if I bring plus two rather than plus one.”

“This isn’t India, Rahul. This type of thing isn’t so casual here.”

Rahul pulled out his phone. “I’m texting my agent now. He’ll take care of it.”

"Your agent is coming?" Her agent couldn't even get her a ticket let alone get himself invited.

"I told you that agent of yours is a dud. I don't understand why you don't sign with mine."

Saira sighed. "Because your agent would only take me because I'm your wife."

Rahul shrugged. "So?"

Mia turned to her. "Rahul's agent has a much bigger agency. He can probably do better for you."

Anger bubbled in her veins. She wagged a finger at both of them. "See, this is why I don't want you two scheming."

Rahul put an arm around her and kissed her head. "*Aare yaar*, we love you, and we want what's best for you."

Saira looked at Mia, who was studiously looking at her shoes. Had she said something to Rahul about loving her?

"Thank you for the party invitation, but I'm afraid I can't go. I have a lot of work to do and nothing to wear."

Rahul put both hands on her shoulders. Mia startled and Saira smiled. Rahul's friendliness took getting used to. "Work can wait, and Saira has plenty of clothes. I think you two are roughly the same size. If you don't like what she has, I'm sure your costume shop can come up with something."

Mia began shaking her head, but Rahul wasn't to be deterred. "We are not leaving without you. Go get your purse and whatever else you need. We'll stop by the hotel, pick up what you and Saira need, then go to my friend's house in the Hills to get dressed. My assistant will arrange for a hairdresser and makeup artist to meet us there."

"I really don't need all that I can do my own..." Mia's protests were completely drowned by Rahul's continued chatter. Saira smiled. It would be nice to see Mia all dressed up. She had just the dress in mind as well. It was one she hadn't yet worn and would look perfect on Mia.

When they got to the hotel, Mia seemed too overwhelmed with the clothes crammed into the small hotel closets, so Saira picked the dress.

Ned Hawkins's bungalow was a cute two-bedroom, three-bath modern house with a fantastic view of downtown LA. It had a step-down living room, open kitchen, and sliding French doors that led to a lap pool and hot tub. The living room walls were decorated with framed movie posters of Ned. Rahul had mentioned that this was Ned's "poor house," the one that he'd bought after he had to sell his mansion. Apparently, he'd never accounted for the fact that leading roles in movies decreased as age increased. To Saira, the house was perfect. Spacious enough for parties but cozy enough for a family. She and Mia could have a house like this, one bedroom for the kids, and one for them.

"How is Ned?" Saira asked. She'd heard rumors on set that he was being hounded by the media as a home-wrecker.

Rahul shook his head. "I talked to him yesterday. The poor guy thought that after George came out, they could finally be together, but it's actually harder for them to even see each other with the tabloid reporters following them everywhere. Plus, George is in a messy divorce, and his lawyer told him to keep away from Ned for now."

They only had a half hour before the hair and makeup people showed up. and Saira did not want to waste a minute of alone time. She pulled Mia into Ned's bedroom. Rahul was using the guest room.

"I feel bad for the guy but he's a little vain, isn't he?" The bedroom walls were littered with headshots of Ned through the years. Saira found a hook at the back of the door and hung up the dresses she had brought for Mia, who was furiously texting on her phone.

She grabbed the phone from Mia's hand. "How about we focus on having fun tonight."

Mia sighed. "I have a lot of work to do."

Saira pulled Mia into her arms and kissed the spot between her neck and ear that drove Mia crazy. Sure enough, goose bumps filled her skin, and Saira ran her hands down her arms as she whispered in her ear, letting her lips brush against Mia's skin. "We won't stay long at the party, and afterwards, we'll go to my hotel and order room service for dessert. How about it?"

Mia wrapped her arms around Saira and

pulled her close. Her mouth found Saira's lips, her hands slid beneath the tank top she'd thrown on after the shoot. She was wearing a bandeau bra and it didn't take long for Mia to push it over her breasts and find her nipples, rolling them between her thumbs. Saira deepened the kiss, her body eager for Mia's touch. Her own hands worked the belt on Mia's cargo pants, pushing them down along with her panties. Mia was so slick that Saira slid two fingers inside her, her own body responding to her lover's moans. Saira knew what Mia wanted. She broke the kiss and stepped back, then put the fingers she'd just had inside Mia in her mouth, tasting Mia's juices. Mia's eyes darkened.

She pulled down her jeans, chucked off her top and bra. Saira followed with her clothes. They came together at the same time, mouths hungry, breasts crushing against each other, hands exploring with fervor. Saira pushed Mia onto the bed, then grabbed her purse, pulling out Mia's favorite sex toy.

"Is that..." Mia's eyes went wide.

Saira nodded. "You left it in my hotel room in Fiji."

"I hope you've gotten good use out of it."

"It's a little hard to enjoy without you." She inserted one side of the double-headed penis inside her, then put the other side inside Mia, watching with pleasure as her head rolled back and she bit her lip. Saira moved on top of her, changing positions ever so slightly, her hand on Mia's stomach to balance herself. She tried but failed to control her own orgasm as Mia squeezed her breasts, rolled her nipples between her fingers and pressed and teased her core with her thumb.

She didn't count the times Mia orgasmed. It was hard enough to keep track of her own as years of pent-up desire and sexual frustration exploded out of her. It wasn't as if she hadn't had sex, not as if she hadn't used the toy, not as if she hadn't orgasmed with her other partners. But it was different with Mia, always had been. There was a freedom in her release, a connection with Mia that she'd tried to achieve with others and never had. It was as if there was an invisible string that connected their hearts and souls and the physical part of their relationship just allowed them to pull that string taut until they were joined together.

Afterward they lay there spent, entwined in each other's arms, kissing and touching, making up for years of missing each other's touch.

Rahul eventually knocked on the door. "I don't hear any moaning and screaming, so hoping you guys are done. The makeup and hair people have been waiting for an hour."

"Be out in a minute," Saira yelled. They both looked at each other and laughed. Saira glanced at her wristwatch and gasped. "Oh, my God, we've been in here for an hour." They'd lost track of time talking and holding each other.

They decided to take a shower separately, knowing that if they did it together, it would be another two hours before they emerged. When Saira emerged from the bathroom, Mia had already put on the dress that she'd brought for her. It was a silky, royal blue, one-shoulder dress that ended just above her knees. The hairdresser was busy getting Mia's short locks pinned so they framed her face in curls. She looked stunning. If

Rahul hadn't gone through all this trouble to make the night special for them, she would've begged off, dragged Mia back into the bedroom.

Saira wore a shimmering silver dress in a twenties flapper style that ended midthigh. They were short on time so she settled for her hair in a quick updo and minimal makeup. Rahul looked stylish in designer jeans, an open collar shirt and a Balenciaga jacket. By the end, even Mia was excited about the night.

A limo took them the twenty minutes up the hills to the mansion where the party was being held. Mia stepped out in the heels that Saira had lent her and pulled down her dress. Luckily the paparazzi were not allowed past the gates. Saira and Rahul had waved to them from the window of the limo, while Mia did her best to slink as far down in her seat as possible. After being checked in by the security guard up front, they entered the foyer where they were greeted with hundreds of LED balloons floating in the ceiling, which created a mesmerizing starry night effect. Rahul's agent found them immediately. Saira turned to Mia. "Do you mind if I make the rounds with Rahul real quick? I need to get some selfies onto insta."

Mia nodded. She needed a few minutes to adjust to the party, and there were several emails that she needed to respond to. The bar was packed, so she picked up a pink cocktail that a waiter was passing on a tray and found a table on the terrace overlooking the pool. It was a cool night and most of the guests were inside, networking, socializing, gossiping. It wasn't her scene. Every now and then, she caught sight of Rahul and Saira, arm in arm, laughing, smiling, posing for photos. They were both so natural at it. Could she ever fit into Saira's world? It felt nice to dress up for a night, pretend she was going to the prom, but it wasn't something that felt natural.

When they were alone, everything seemed so easy, like they belonged together. But every time she stepped outside their cocoon, Mia was hit with the reality that Saira lived in a different world than she did. Saira was used to having hairdressers and makeup artists come to her house to get her ready for a party. Wearing designer clothes, air-kissing people, nibbling on little toasts with dribbles of sauce on them and calling it food—it wasn't something Mia could get used to. The dress she was wearing itched her skin, the pins in her hair hurt, the heels pinched her feet and she was starving. She'd taken five of the last set of cute square thingies that the waiter had passed. It took stuffing two of them in her mouth at one time to figure out it was something with crab in it. She'd drunk four screwdrivers just for the orange juice.

How would they ever make it work? Saira wouldn't be happy going to these parties alone, and Mia wasn't sure she could bring herself to do this on a daily basis. She stared as Rahul and Saira posed with the party hosts, a celebrity couple who would definitely bring some attention to their social media posts. Would Saira ever want to give up the fame and adoration? She was doing it to support her family but she also enjoyed the attention; it was clear in the way her face lit up every time someone asked to take a selfie with her.

"You in love with him or her?"

She turned to find herself staring into the brown eyes of Rahul's agent. Steve Machelan was wearing a funky plaid green suit that made him look like a dressed-up leprechaun. He gestured to the empty chair beside her, and she felt rude not nodding even though she had no desire to make small talk.

"I'm Steve by the way." He held out his hand and she took it, returning his warm smile.

"I know. I'm Mia." Despite his tragic sense of dress, Steve had a nice smile. He had a Southern California tan, well-styled sandy brown hair and perfectly white teeth.

"So, you in love with him or her?"

"I'm not in love with either of them. I'm producing her show."

"I know. *Life with Meera.* Rahul had me call in quite a number of favors to get you the gig."

She looked at him. "I didn't ask her to do that."

He quirked a brow. "Then why did she do it?"

Mia shrugged. "We were friends a long

time ago. She had some issues with the show and knew I'd do a good job."

Why am I even talking to this guy. It's none of his business.

As if he'd read her mind, he leaned forward. "Rahul loves his wife. I suspect he loves her in the way one best friend loves another."

Mia stayed silent. She had no idea what Rahul's agent did or didn't know, and she was not in the habit of accidentally outing people.

"He wants me to take Saira on as a client, and I'd be happy to. She's talented and has a lot of potential. If *Life with Meera* is a hit, she'll have a lot of options. But...." He paused, as if waiting for her to fill in the blanks. Mia stared at him expectantly. She wasn't going to give him anything. He wanted to talk to her, he could keep up the conversation.

"But, I worry that their personal lives are about to implode."

Mia kept her face impassive but her pulse raced. What was Steve talking about?

He slid his phone toward her, and Mia

gasped. On his screen was a photo of her and Saira from a few hours ago. They were both naked, their entire bodies on full display, Saira's hand between her legs, Mia's hand on her breast, their mouths devouring each other. The picture wasn't grainy; someone had taken it from fairly close range. Neither Mia nor Saira had paid attention to the windows in that room.

"I make it a point to have a full-time staff member who has just one task—to keep an eye on all the websites where freelance photographers—I refuse to call them journalists—put up pictures for sale. Know the sale price for these?"

Mia's stomach churned.

"It's five thousand dollars."

What?

"You're a nobody and the photographer didn't recognize Saira. He was after Ned Hawkins, hoping to get a picture of him and George. I was able to negotiate him down to two thousand."

Mia breathed a sigh of relief.

"But that doesn't mean that he, or someone else, won't be back. Two thousand for a couple hours' worth of work is good enough for most of these guys."

Mia's throat was dry. She took a gulp of the pink cocktail and coughed as the sickly-sweet liquid went down her throat.

"So tell me, Mia, was this just a one-night stand, or do I need to worry that my client's marriage is about to end?"

Mia took another sip of the horrible drink, looking away from the picture on the phone.

Steve leaned forward. "I'm only looking out for their best interest."

She very much doubted that. He was looking out for his best interest, to get ahead of any issue that would affect his ability to get top dollar for his client, and therefore himself.

"What do you want me to say or do?"

He took his phone back. "I want you to tell me whether Rahul knows you're having an affair with his wife."

She nodded. There was no harm in acknowledging that.

"Is he gay?"

She looked up in surprise.

"Oh, don't give me that wide-eyed look.

They won't be the first closeted celebrity couple."

"I'm done talking with you."

She pushed her chair back but he placed his hand on top of hers. "You don't have to talk to me. But hear me out. Rahul is at the top of his career right now. So is Saira. I understand she wants to work in LA. She can do that, bright future ahead and all that. But, not if she comes out. Not right now. I'm negotiating a major contract for Rahul, a part in an upcoming superhero movie. No matter how woke we all are, he won't get the part if he comes out right now. If Rahul makes it, Saira's career will follow. They are as lovable as Harry and Megan. Don't ruin it for them."

Thirteen

Saira tried to keep an eye on Mia. Why wouldn't she come join them? She'd been sitting by herself on the lawn, nursing the same drink for the last hour. As she posed for a picture, she was glad to see Steve approach her. Maybe he would convince her to join the party. Despite how she hadn't wanted to come to this party, Saira was enjoying herself. The crowd was very different from Mumbai. People talked about art, literature, the industry. Gossip and fashion were staples in LA as well as Mumbai, but Saira found herself enjoying being a new face on the social circuit. People wanted to talk to her, get to know her. At least one director and two producers had asked for her agent's name.

As much as she hated to admit it, she liked the adoration. When she was with her family, the conversation revolved around Kayra. Even before Kayra's illness, dinner talks were filled with questions about whether she had memorized her lines, what offers had come her way, which movies were currently casting and how best to position her to get the parts. Her publicist, agent and staff were always focused on what was wrong with her—is that a pimple starting on your face? Did you eat dessert last night, because there's an extra centimeter on your waistline. It was only when she was with her fans when she felt that somebody appreciated how hard she worked. It took her hours to memorize her lines for every day of shooting. If the scene was complicated, she practiced with her assistants. She prided herself on showing up to every shoot prepared to act well enough for one take.

Mia was still sitting at the same outside table she'd seen her at almost an hour ago.

Why wasn't she enjoying this? Mia loved to talk art, literature, politics, pretty much any topic you threw at her. Why was she sitting in the corner sulking like someone had given her a sour Popsicle?

Once they were done taking pictures, she turned to Rahul. "I'm going to go see if Mia is okay."

He nodded absently as he continued his conversation with a director about some superhero role they were negotiating. Maybe Rahul was right, perhaps she should take advantage of his offer and sign with Steve. It had been Rahul introducing her to Peter Denton at a party that had gotten her the part for *Life with Meera*. Her agent had just negotiated the deal, he hadn't found it for her. Steve, on the other hand, was constantly bringing offers to Rahul. It was Rahul who turned them down. Always because of a man. Hosiang was in Tibet, which was much closer to India than California. Before Hosiang there had been London-based Norris. What if Rahul hadn't turned down the offers from LA? What if he had become a Hollywood A-lister rather than a Bollywood one? He could have come out, lived his life openly.

By the time she wove through the crowd, Mia was no longer there. She approached Steve, who was still sitting at the table.

"Where did Mia go?"

He shrugged. "Saira, can we talk for a second? There's something I need to show you."

The picture stopped her cold. How could she have been so stupid? The first thing she did when she entered a room was drop the curtains. She closed her eyes, not wanting the beautiful memory of being with Mia to be tainted by the sleazy-looking picture.

"I've taken care of this picture. But you need to be more careful."

Saira nodded. There was nothing else she could say. She had been stupid and careless.

"Thank you, Steve. I'll pay you back..."

He waved her off. "It was a minor expense. Trust me, it could've been worse. Pictures like these go for tens of thousands of dollars, in the hundreds of thousands if you're an A-lister. That's why these guys spend so much time stalking all of the houses in the Hills."

She turned to Steve. “Can I ask you for some career advice?”

“Don’t come out now.”

“Are you telling me this as Rahul’s agent?”

“I’m advising you based on twenty years of experience as an agent in LA.” He put a hand on her arm. “LA is not Mumbai. You’re not going to be vilified for being a lesbian. Most people will celebrate your courage in coming out. You will get some backlash from some members of the LGBTQ community for being ashamed of your identity and perpetuating the belief that you need to be straight in order to succeed in life. But that can be countered with a narrative about how you are now standing up against the heteronormative culture in India and showing your courage in coming out.” Now that he had her attention, he picked up his drink, a whiskey on the rocks from the look and smell, and took a sip before continuing.

“You’re at the top of your career but from here, the slope is downhill. You’ve got a few more big movies, maybe a couple of TV series. After that, you’ll be limited to roles specifically written for you, and those are rare. If you come out now, you'll get a lot of media attention, but it won't be good for your prospects. That saying—there is no such thing as bad press—is totally wrong. Movie financiers want a sure thing. They don't want a potentially controversial figure who the public can't buy in the role that she's portraying. I can't sell you for a lead part in a male-female rom-com if you are constantly in the press as the poster child for gay rights. I can't even sell you as the girl next door if the boy is going to be interested in her."

Saira took a breath. "So much for LA being more tolerant."

"It is better than most parts of the world. You're not going to get stoned to death for being a lesbian. You can live openly and freely. But yeah, we're a lot less liberal than we claim to be. It's one of those things no one talks about. We pretend we're above the rest of the world, that we promote gay rights. If you look at the well-known actors and actresses who're out, they are front and center at parties, talk shows and award ceremonies—but not in leading roles on the big screen. Movies have to appeal to a broad audience, and that includes parts of America where being gay is considered a sin."

Saira's legs were so weak, she didn't know if she could stand on them. This whole time, she had counted on the fact that LA was a way out for her, that she could build a new life. But if she couldn't support her family, then how could she leave Mumbai? How could she make a life with Mia?

Fourteen

Could she call an Uber from a celebrity mansion? Mia stood at the doorstep debating how to get out to the front gate when Saira caught up to her. "I've been looking everywhere for you."

"I need to go home."

"Is everything okay?"

Mia looked around. There were so many people milling about, taking pictures, cell phones at the ready. "I think that pink cocktail doesn't agree with me. I feel a little sick."

Saira pressed her lips, then pulled out her phone. "I'm calling Rahul to send the driver for us."

"No, you should stay, enjoy the party. You need to network. I think I saw Steven Spielberg and Kevin Blum earlier."

Saira hesitated. It was just for a second, but enough for Mia to see the want in Saira's eyes. She squeezed her arm. "I'll take the car. Text me when the party's over."

Saira shook her head. "I'd rather spend the time with you."

The odd tone of Saira's voice rang a little alarm for Mia, but she couldn't pay attention to it with Saira looking at her like she was her entire world.

They rode in silence to the hotel. Once there, they spent the night making love, both of them hungry and eager and making up for lost years. They slept naked under the sheets, and this time when Mia held Saira, there was nothing platonic or comforting about it. It was late morning when they woke up to the hotel doorbell. Mia glanced at her wristwatch and startled at how late it was. She was used to waking up before dawn.

As Saira put on a robe to open the door, Mia checked her emails. Several from David with a bunch of tedious things she needed to take care of, one from Chris, asking her to prepare a pitch for the streaming services by tomorrow. At least the social media campaign was working. #LifeWithMeera wasn't big nationally but it was trending locally, which meant a lot in LA.

The sound of a metal trolley and the popping of a champagne bottle got Mia out of bed. She threw on the hotel robe and walked into the living room to see a room service trolley with a scrumptious-looking breakfast, a bottle of Cristal champagne and chocolate-covered strawberries laid out on the table.

"Where did all this come from?"

Saira waved to a note that the waiter had placed on the coffee table, picking up a chocolate-covered strawberry. "Rahul must have sent it. He does stuff like this all the time. Especially after he makes me pose for a million photos."

Mia wanted to say something but kept her mouth shut. Rahul was a genuinely nice person, but Saira couldn't see that he too was using her, like everyone else in her life.

Saira held out a strawberry. "I'll share."

Mia smiled and took a bite as Saira held out the strawberry, letting her mouth suck and lick Saira's fingers. She pulled Saira into a hug. "We were young in Fiji, unsettled in our lives, unsure of ourselves. We're not those people anymore. We can figure this out, Saira. We can figure out how to be together."

Saira nodded, then pulled out of her arms. "I am starving, and even the five-star hotels in India haven't quite figured out how to make pancakes, so I'm going to enjoy these while I'm here."

She sat at the table and added two pancakes to her plate from the stack. Mia picked up the card on the table and opened it. Her stomach turned. "Breakfast isn't from Rahul," she said dryly.

Saira raised her brows. "Well, are you going to tell me or keep me in suspense?"

"Steve sent this."

Saira stopped midchew, then recovered. She set down her fork. "I meant to tell you last night but we…um…got caught up with other things. I've decided to fire my agent and sign with Steve."

Mia's stomach turned even more.

"What made you change your mind?"

"I bumped into him at the party and he gave me some advice. I found it useful and realized that he knows Hollywood a lot better than my agent. He'll be better able to navigate it for me."

Mia's mouth was dry. She picked up a glass of orange juice and nearly downed half of it. She herself had suggested that Saira sign with Steve. But that was before her conversation with him at the party. "Did he show you the pictures?"

Saira stared at her for what seemed like forever. "He showed the pictures to you too?"

Mia nodded. "With a warning to stay away from you and not ruin your career. And Rahul's too."

Saira sighed. "He said something similar to me." She reached out her arm and grabbed Mia's hand. "Look, I'm not blindly following his advice. Unlike my agent, he's got a better network of contacts to help me land roles, and he's got a whole staff that does public relations. Not all agents offer that type of full service."

"I'm not arguing that he's a good agent. What I'm wondering is why you selected him, knowing he won't support you living your life openly. He made it pretty clear that he thought you and Rahul should stay firmly in the closet."

"That doesn't mean we're going to listen to him. Rahul and I are on the same page that we're tired of living our life in secret, constantly afraid of being outed, considering each partner with suspicion. We're just trying to be smart about how we manage our careers so we don't end up like those stars who get invited to every party but don't have the money to buy a dress."

Mia pushed her plate of eggs away, her appetite gone. Those last words were not Saira's, but Steve's.

Saira moved and knelt next to her. She took both of Mia's hands in her own. "I'm going to find a way for us to be together, openly. But it's going to take time. I have to see what roles Steve can get me, develop a financial plan, talk to my family… There's a lot I have to do. I need you to be patient with me….please."

It all made perfect sense. It hadn't even been a week since that day in the costume room when she first saw Saira. So much had happened that neither of them had had time to sit back and think or reflect.

She nodded and kissed Saira lightly on the lips. But the alarm bells in her head were loudly clanging.

Weeks later, *Life with Meera* wasn't completely off the chopping block but the knives had been set down. One of the streaming giants agreed to pick it up after seeing a clip from the first day of filming. As Mia suspected, Saira's charm and talent shone through the screen. But they were still on the hook to get filming finished in six weeks, and they were currently running two days behind schedule.

Mia slung her messenger bag across her shoulder; she needed to hurry to make it to the studio. She'd spent all morning stuck in meetings, and now it was almost lunch time and she and Saira had a routine. Six weeks had gone by since she and Saira had taken up together, but they still couldn't get enough of each other. Mia didn't spend every night with Saira, especially not after her makeup artist and David had complained about the puffiness under her eyes, but they did eat lunch and dinner together when they could. Mia had cooked for Saira a couple of times, and then there was room service. Mia barely slept five hours each night but she didn't care. She had waited for ten years to be with Saira and was going to savor every second.

As soon as she entered the studio, she knew something was wrong. According to the schedule, they should be in the middle of taping but everyone looked to be on break. The actors were nowhere to be seen, the camera crew and staff were scattered about, many at the catering table, which hadn't yet been set up for lunch.

David found Mia just as she began searching for him. "We have a problem."

"Clearly. What's going on?"

"You need to rein Saira in. She requested more script changes…" Mia nodded. She had started to go over those with Saira yesterday, but it had been in Mia's bedroom and they'd gotten distracted before finishing the full review.

"The other actors are getting frustrated. They get changes the night before, they don't have enough time to relearn their lines. We were on the sixth take for the last scene when I sent everyone to their trailers to go learn the lines."

Mia sighed. She'd been afraid of this. "Saira has script approval."

"I know. But at the end of today, we're going to be three days behind. It's not just the script changes. Saira isn't coming prepared. She needs constant reminding of her lines. We've been running late for the last week and everyone is tired. Saturday was supposed to be a half day but I need to extend it to catch up."

"I'll talk to her."

David shook his head. "I've already talked to her." He leaned in conspiratorially. "I heard that she's having an affair, and that's why she's so distracted."

Mia went cold. After the pictures that Steve had bought, she and Saira had been so careful. They never entered her hotel together. Mia had even figured out an entrance through the parking lot that was less public. For their afternoon romps, Mia always knocked loudly on her door and announced that she needed to go over script changes, or went to her dressing room before Saira and left after. The window shades were always drawn and white noise turned up high.

"David, you know better than to listen to set gossip."

He shook his head. "It's not just the gossip about the affair. I think she's busy preparing for another project. I was at a dinner last night and—" he looked around to make sure no one was in listening range "—one of my fellow directors… I can't name names… he said that he was casting for a movie and Saira's name came up. But her agent said that she wasn't available to read for the part because she was busy preparing for some big Bollywood project."

Her mouth soured. She had to admit that they didn't seem to have much time to talk between Saira's filming schedule and Mia's meetings, but Saira would have told her if she signed on to some big Bollywood project. Wouldn't she? How many times had she mentioned the various roles that Steve had found for her? She had even read for a supporting actress role in a major film. Saira hadn't gotten the part.

David was looking at her expectantly. Mia sighed. "It's really none of our business what Saira is doing. But her performance on our show is something we should address, and I will."

"You do that. We need to right this ship now."

Mia made her way to Saira's dressing room. Saira greeted her like she aways did, with a kiss that made Mia forget why she'd come in the first place. She pulled away.

"We need to talk."

"Uh-oh."

"David's upset."

Saira nodded. "I know. And he's right. I've been messing up my lines, and today I forgot half my actions too. I sat down when I was supposed to be pacing and clapped by hands when I was supposed to slap my forehead."

"That's not like you."

Saira nodded. "Just been so stressed lately.

I'm reading a ton of scripts, plus there's all this social stuff."

"Something's got to give. You've been going out three or four times a night. Can you skip the parties?" She kept her voice neutral. She didn't want to come across as the nagging girlfriend.

Saira sighed. "Steve thinks it's important I network in LA." She reached over and ran a finger down Mia's arm. "Then there's making sure I keep you happy." Her tone was teasing but Mia caught the stress between the words.

"We don't have to spend so much time together. I've been falling behind on my work too. I had to stay up until 3:00 a.m. last night just to get through my emails and invoice approvals."

Saira shook her head and pulled Mia into her arms. "No. That's the one thing we can't compromise on. You and I have waited so long to be together. We can't let the pressures of daily life keep us away from each other."

Mia nodded but her stomach was in a thousand knots as she looked at Saira. How had she not noticed the bags under her eyes, the paleness of her skin under the cream-colored foundation.

"Why don't I leave you to go over the lines for the afternoon taping."

"It's almost lunch. Are you sure you don't want to stay?" Saira ran a hand up her thigh and Mia's body responded immediately. She could spare some time, couldn't she? They could be quick.

She placed a hand on top of Saira's. "You need to practice your lines, and I need to go smooth things over with David."

Saira did that thing with her lips that was somewhere between a pout and a smirk, and it took every ounce of Mia's self-control to leavc.

By week ten, they were six days behind on their taping schedule. David was ready to quit; one of the writers had already thrown a fit and walked off. The crew was upset because they had been working overtime, and everyone's temper was on the last string.

"No more script changes!" David screamed

at her. They were in Mia's office, having just met with the editing staff. She and David had both missed an inconsistency between episode one and five.

"To be fair, David, neither one of us, or the writers caught that we had to change the episode five script."

"A problem we wouldn't have to deal with if we weren't wholesale rewriting the script as we tape."

"You were in love with the script changes. I'm the one who had a problem with it."

"For about thirty seconds, then you started sleeping with Saira and lost all control over the show."

Mia froze. *How does he know?* "That's a rude accusation."

David crossed his arms. "It's not an accusation—it's a statement of fact. You think no one notices that you two hole up in her trailer at lunch, and both of you come out looking all flushed and smelling of sex?"

Her face heated. Did everyone on set know? How could she have been so careless? Her reputation would be ruined. It was one thing to have an affair on set, it was another when their relationship was being blamed for the star's performance.

"Don't worry. The only people who know are Gail, my assistant, and me. We've done our best to quash the talk. Gail even went as far as to tell people that you're dating someone else."

Mia sank into a chair. There was no point in denying it. David pulled out the guest chair and sat opposite her. "Why are you protecting me?" It would've been so much easier for David to let the rumors take hold and have the network fire her. He'd been wanting to call Saira's agent and threaten nonperformance on the contract if she didn't improve. Mia had stopped him. Then he'd wanted to call a meeting with the network executives and change the schedule. Production delays happened on every show and film—it wasn't that unusual a request. But Mia had dug her heels in. She was still afraid the network would cancel the show.

David rolled his eyes. "Believe me, I'd like nothing more than to throw you to the wolves. But you're one of the best producers I've worked with. You're not a network ass-kisser, you care about the quality of the show and you don't try to blow smoke up my ass when something isn't working."

Mia smiled. It was actually quite a compliment coming from David.

"What do I need to do?"

He put up four fingers. "First, you need to tell Saira that she gets one last go at script changes. All of them need to be turned in in a day or two. That'll give us some time to review the changes and make sure we don't have more mistakes that require reshooting."

Mia nodded. It was a reasonable request, and if she hadn't been so busy with her head between Saira's thighs, she would have insisted on that a long time ago.

"Second, you need to get us more time with the network. I need two extra weeks. We can make up the time in editing."

Mia bit her lip. "It'll be tough getting time on the actor's calendars."

"We can work around that. There are a number of solo scenes with Saira. As long as we have her, I can make the schedule work."

"The bigger issue is the budget for the crew's time."

David nodded. "That's an issue you're going to have to solve. I'll do my best to go with a skeleton crew, but you're still going to have to convince the network weenies to open their wallets."

Mia nodded. She had already calculated a week of extra budget and had a proposal ready, but that was if they had no further delays, which was wishful thinking.

"Third, you're going to give the crew the entire weekend plus Friday afternoon off."

Mia opened her mouth but David shook his head. "Don't protest. Everyone is exhausted and making stupid mistakes. They need a break. I've baked that into the time extension."

Again, Mia nodded. These were all things she'd been thinking about anyway.

"Last, you're going to break it off with Saira."

Mia froze.

"I'm not saying forever. Just until we finish filming. You are a distraction and we're at a critical point now. We can't afford to waste time. Plus, it's only a matter of time before everyone finds out. Unless she's ready to come out of the closet, it's not fair for you to keep at it."

As much as she hated to admit it, David was right.

Fifteen

Saira rubbed her temples, closing her eyes with the hope that her headache would disappear. She had too much work to do. Mia had asked for all remaining script changes by tomorrow. On top of that, Mia hadn't had lunch or dinner with her, begging off with some excuse about meetings. She was a horrible liar. There was something going on. Had she found out about the Mumtaz Mahal role? Saira had been in discussions with the movie producers; they were offering 8 percent above her regular fee. It wasn't just the money. The role was amazing. She'd get to play a tragic historical character who inspired an iconic monument of love. The movie had international blockbuster written all over it. Even Steve was encouraging her to do it.

Saira had been hoping Steve would come up with a better option for her in LA. He had done better than her last agent but also given her the same advice that she needed to wait for *Life with Meera* to come out. There was some nice buzz about the show, but because Saira was still untested with American audiences, the offers coming in were limited to supporting roles that didn't pay even a quarter of what Bollywood was offering.

She had to discuss the Mumtaz Mahal role with Mia, but every time she tried to bring it up, the thought of how Mia would react stopped her. Their entire relationship felt as though it was held together by cello tape. Any day now, one piece would get ripped off and the whole thing would collapse. Mia said she was trying to give her the time she needed to figure things out, but not a day went by when Mia didn't ask whether she'd heard from Steve, or when she planned to talk to her family. How did she make Mia understand all the pressures that were on her? On top of everything, Kayra wanted Saira to come see her. Even if she used Rahul's private jet subscription, it was twelve hours each way. They were already behind schedule on filming, a fact that was stressing Mia out. Saira couldn't ask for extra days to go visit her sister.

She grabbed her purse and shook out two paracetamol tablets, washing them down with the can of soda sitting on her bedside table.

She looked at the WhatsApp message from Kayra.

I really need to see you, di. There's something important I want to discuss with the family. I can't do it without you.

What could it be? The last time Kayra had a request, it was to permanently stay at the Swiss center. Had she found another place, or did she want to come home? She had tried calling Kayra, but all she would say over video is that she wanted to talk to Saira in person. Her mother had no idea what was going on; all she said was that Saira had to find a way to go visit Kayra.

In the meantime, she had an impossible deadline for script changes, and she still had to learn her lines for the next day. Maybe it was a good thing that Mia hadn't come over. No matter how hard Saira tried, it was difficult to focus on anything when she was with Mia. She had fallen behind on so many important tasks: reviewing her accountant's reports, reading the new scripts from both her agents, learning her lines. All Saira wanted to do was be with Mia, spend time with her, suck up every last ounce of her. But that didn't leave much time for anything else.

Her phone buzzed with a call from Rahul. He was filming in Greece. She put the phone on Speaker.

"Isn't it the middle of the night there?" she said when she answered.

"Yes, but I miss my wife. I had to talk to her."

"You do know there is no one listening on this line."

"It's the truth, *yaar*. I do miss you. What happened with Jay is really troubling me."

She sat up. "What happened with Jay?"

"You didn't hear?"

She shook her head, then realized they were on a voice call. "No. I haven't been looking at the news back home. Too busy."

He sighed. "I hope you're sitting down."

She was, but she pulled a pillow closer and hugged it tight. Jay Goshal was a prominent director, and a really nice guy. Saira had worked with him on six projects. "He was leaving his apartment complex in Bandra, just getting ready to meet his driver in the garage, when a worker—I think it was a gardener or something—approached him and threw acid in his face."

"Oh, my God! No! Is he okay?" Bile rose in the back of her throat and her stomach heaved. She clutched the pillow to her stomach and doubled over it.

"Half his face, neck and the top of his shoulder are badly burned. He's still in the ICU. For security reasons, they won't disclose what hospital he's in. Last I heard, he'll make it, but it's going to be a long road to recovery."

"Give me a second."

She rushed to the bathroom and made it just in time as the meager contents of her stomach came up her throat. She could hear Rahul calling out to her from the speaker.

She returned to the bed.

"Are you okay?"

"What the hell, Rahul? How did this happen?"

"The guy who did it was a nutjob. Apparently, his only son just told him he was gay and Jay was his idol or something. He wanted to be a director. The father snapped, got a job in the apartment complex. You know how these guys are—they blame the celebrity for their problems, thinking by hurting us, they're somehow solving their own problems."

"No, they're punishing us. They think we're the ones to blame for whatever is affecting their personal lives. I mean, if Jay isn't safe in his own home, what hope do we have?"

"India's not ready yet, Saira. It's getting there, but not yet."

"How long, Rahul? Are we going to have

to wait for our children's generation to be able to live openly?"

"I don't know. Look, it's not all bad. I mean, there was *Chandigarh di Aashiqui*—that movie where Vaani Kapoor played the transgender woman. . . ."

"Yeah, a nice movie, except that Abhishek didn't cast a trans woman to play the role. Instead, he chose Vaani, who did a nice job, but she's not trans." Saira had been approached about that role but had declined it because she'd felt that a trans woman should play the role.

"See, that's what I mean. It's changing but not fully there. Next time, they'll cast a trans woman. Look, Sonam Kapoor played a lesbian in *Ek Ladki Ko Dekha*. There's hope. Hey, imagine if you had taken that role?"

Saira wished she had. The movie was about a woman who had to come out to her traditional family in order to marry the woman she loved. It was only four years ago, but her parents had talked her out of taking the role. Kayra had finally been settled and happy and they didn't want her affected by any backlash.

"I wish I had. It would make it so much easier to come out."

"You're not still thinking of doing that, are you? Not after what happened with Jay?"

"How long are we going to wait, Rahul? It's never going to end, is it? There will always be someone dangerous out there." But even as she said the words, her stomach heaved. It was one thing to put herself at risk, but what if they came after her family? Kayra was safe in Switzerland and Mia was in America, but what about her parents?

They were both silent for a while, then Rahul spoke, "Hosiang said he's decided to leave the monastery. Being with me has made him realize that he has unresolved issues and he needs to figure them out."

"Are you getting back together with him?"

"He didn't betray me on purpose."

"It's not fair to him. He's trying to confront his truth and you're telling him to hide and lie for you."

"It's not by choice."

"Isn't it?" That's what Mia kept telling her. It was a choice. Not an easy one but it was a choice. Mia had lost her parents. It hadn't been easy for her to live openly—it wasn't as if she'd gotten the acceptance she wanted—but she hadn't taken the easy path.

As if reading her mind, Rahul sighed deeply. "If you're thinking about Mia, she had more of a choice than we do. Yes, she had to fight against her parents, but you and I both know that if it was just about standing up to our parents, we would do it. Mia doesn't get thrown out of her job for being a lesbian. She doesn't risk her livelihood, she doesn't worry every time she leaves her house that a seemingly innocent servant will throw acid in her face. I mean look at Ned—he had to stay away from his own house for months because he was being called a home wrecker."

Tears stung her eyes. "How arc we ever going to be happy?"

"*Yaar,* I called you 'cause I was feeling low, and now we're both even lower."

"That's life, Rahul."

She hung up with him and closed her eyes, her stomach still heaving. How was she ever going to keep her family safe if she came out? How was she going to be with Mia? Her head hurt. She needed time to figure it all out. Was Rahul right? Was this just something she couldn't have in her lifetime and should just hope that her children could have it in the future?

Her laptop pinged with another email. It was daytime in India and people were waiting on answers. A little time. That's all she needed. Some space to catch up with everything she had to do so she could think clearly, figure out how she was going to sort out her life.

It was early morning by the time she finished with the script changes. She was tired and had to be on set in four hours. She had to get some sleep if she was going to be functional.

The next day just got worse. Saira had such a headache that she couldn't remember her lines. David sent her home. Mia was nowhere to be seen, supposedly in meetings with the network.

Saira had several emails from her Bollywood agent. She needed to make a commitment to the Mumtaz Mahal role. He'd managed to convince them to give her 8.5

percent above her normal asking fee. Nine months wasn't that long of a time to be away from Mia. *Maybe we can find a way to make it work. I can fly here once a month and Mia can come visit.* It was a nice thought, but Saira knew what filming schedules were like. Any free time she had would go toward any number of social events or endorsement deals. Mia would get busy with another project and she wouldn't be able to come. They would grow apart. Could their relationship withstand the distance? Mia understood what Saira was dealing with. She would understand, wouldn't she? If they hadn't moved on from each other in ten years, what was nine months of being apart? Steve had assured her that after *Life with Meera* came out, he'd have better offers for her.

Her accountant sent her a red envelope email. She opened it to find that an unexpected bill had come in from the ashram her mother frequented, and Kayra's facility bill was again higher than normal. He was asking permission to break one of her fixed deposits to cover the payments. Saira rubbed her temples. The fixed deposits were her savings, and she lost money if she broke the deposit before the due date. She looked at the invoice from the ashram but the numbers swam before her eyes. She slammed the laptop lid shut. There weren't enough hours in the day.

A WhatsApp message pinged on her phone. It was Kayra asking whether they could talk. Normally Saira tried to talk to her sister a few times a week, but calls with Kayra took at least an hour and she still had to memorize her lines for tomorrow. She couldn't have another bad day on set. A second later another text came in, this one from Mia, saying she was on her way to the hotel. Saira rubbed her temples. For the first time since she'd come to LA, she was not looking forward to seeing Mia. With Mia there, Saira wouldn't be able to focus on her lines, plus she couldn't keep putting off telling her about the Mumtaz role.

She washed her face and changed her clothes. Mia keyed into the hotel room. Saira knew something was wrong the moment she walked in. It was in the way her smile didn't reach her eyes, in the stiff way she walked and sat down on the couch with her legs crossed. She was wearing a black business suit. Mia hated business suits. She only wore them when she had to. Things must be really bad with the network.

"I'm sorry I didn't get my lines right today. I stayed up all night working on the script changes and didn't get enough sleep."

"So it's my fault?"

"I never said that." Saira went and sat beside Mia. She put a hand on her knee. "What is going on?"

"We need two more weeks to finish the show. The network isn't happy about it, but thankfully it's too late to pull the plug. They *are* going to torture me by giving me a ridiculously small budget in which there is no way I can have all the staff I need to finish filming. I'm going to have to fire Gail."

Saira squeezed her hand. She knew how much Mia valued Gail's friendship. "I am so sorry. But filming was scheduled to end anyway, right, so it's not like you're really firing Gail."

Mia squeezed the bridge of her nose. "Actually, she was supposed to be my assistant through the end of production. But the only way I can make the budget work is to let her go now. Which means more work for me, by the way."

"I am sorry." She didn't know what else to say. Mia seemed miserable, but Saira didn't have a way to make her feel better.

Mia opened her mouth, then closed it.

"You blame me, don't you? This wouldn't have happened if I hadn't screwed up my lines all those times."

Mia shook her head. "This happens on all shows. There are always production delays, the bosses are never happy, and at this point, I'm usually questioning my career choice."

"Then what is it?"

"A few people know about us on the show."

Saira's throat closed. "Who? How?" she choked out.

"It's just David, his assistant and Gail."

Saira's pulse raced. "Gail is a huge gossip. By now the whole crew probably knows."

Once again Mia shook her head. "We can trust David and Gail."

That was easy for Mia to say. She hadn't been betrayed over and over again, nor did she have to worry about what would happen if someone did leak their relationship.

She stood and paced the length of the small living room. "We can't meet in my trailer anymore. And you can't come to the hotel."

Mia was silent. Saira paced some more. How much did Gail and David know? Had they taken any pictures? She turned to Mia. "We should take a break. Just for a little while. Until filming is over."

"That's exactly what David asked me to do."

Saira stopped. "Okay, then we're in agreement."

Mia stood. "Actually, I told him no. I promised that we wouldn't get together while on set, but that our relationship is not up for negotiation." She gave Saira a hard look. "Glad to know where I stand with you."

Saira stepped back, her chest and throat so tight that she wasn't sure if she was even getting enough air. "That's not fair. I can't have our relationship go public now. We've talked about this. You know how much I have at stake."

Mia placed her hands on her hips and Saira stiffened. She knew this posture. "We've talked a lot about what you have at stake, but have you considered that I'm affected too? David has already implied that our relationship is affecting the show, that I've been too soft with you, that I've been distracted. This is a big show for me. I mess this up and I'm going to be stuck doing projects no one else wants. I don't want our relationship getting out any more than you do. But, unlike you, I'm not willing to throw away our relationship every time there's a bump in the road."

She still doesn't understand. They'd been having the same argument since Fiji. Mia saw everything as black and white; either Saira was willing to come out or she wasn't, either she was willing to give up her life in Mumbai or she wasn't; either she loved Mia or she didn't. How many times did she need to ask Mia for more time? Mia knew the position she was in, the stress she was under. Why couldn't she be more understanding?

Saira rubbed her temples. "That's not fair. I didn't say we should break up, I just think that a break might not be a bad idea—to protect us both."

As soon as the words were out of her mouth, Saira knew it was the wrong thing to say. The look on Mia's face sent daggers through her heart.

"Have you ever taken a break from being a daughter or sister?" Mia grabbed her purse and wrenched the door open. "You don't take breaks from the people you love."

Sixteen

The fact that things improved on set only made it harder for Mia. Saira had sent her an apology text and begged her to come back to the hotel room so they could talk. Mia suggested that they take the night to think on it. Saira had appeared on set looking fresh and bright. She'd delivered her lines flawlessly, and David had beamed. Had he been right? Was their relationship affecting Saira's performance? Maybe they had been spending too much time together. She had to admit that having the evening to herself yesterday gave her the time she needed to rework the budget that Chris had requested. She'd figured out a way to pay for two more weeks of the crew's time.

Maybe a break wasn't such a bad idea. Things had been so intense for the last two and a half months, neither of them had any breathing room.

"Can I talk to you?"

How did Saira always manage to sneak up on her? Mia had just finished pouring herself a cup of coffee from the catering table.

They found a quiet corner in the studio. The crew was setting up for the next shot and Saira could get called any second.

"Look, I'm sorry about yesterday. I was stressed about messing up my lines, and I had just been thinking about how there is so much to do and so little time and...."

"And spending less time with me felt like a good way to make space in your day."

"Yes... I mean no. Wait.... just give me a second."

She put a hand through her hair and Mia instinctively reached out to stop her. "Don't ruin your do."

Saira leaned forward. "I love you. I've loved you since the day we met."

David called for the actors. Saira sighed. “Please try and understand where I’m coming from.”

Mia stood rooted as Saira walked away. Saira loved her. They’d said it to each other in Fiji, but that was different. Mia had spent a sleepless night wondering whether Saira was tired of her. Whether Mia had misconstrued really amazing sex for love. Whether she was once again in a one-sided relationship and destined to be left alone.

The day couldn’t end soon enough for her. She kept herself busy in her office, afraid that if she were in the studio with Saira, she wouldn’t be able to resist pulling her into a dark corner or her dressing room. She’d promised David that she would not be distracted during working hours and would leave Saira alone to focus on her lines. He hadn’t been happy that Mia wouldn’t break it off, but she reminded him of the countless relationships that happened on set, including one that he notoriously had with a previous actress. After being pinned in his glass house, he resisted the urge to throw any more stones at her. But that didn’t mean he wouldn't go low and spread rumors if he felt she wasn't keeping up her side of the bargain.

Gail stuck her head in just as Mia was getting ready to leave. "Can I talk to you for a second?"

Mia nodded guiltily. She had yet to break the news to Gail that she wouldn't have a job. She was trying to find a way to keep her, but it wasn't looking good. Mia had put out feelers for other positions. It would be easier to break the news if she had options to give Gail.

Gail sat in the guest chair across from Mia. She clasped her hands. "You can't fire me."

"Excuse me?" It took a second for Mia to process what Gail had said.

"I know you're working the budget, and there's no way you're going to make it work unless you get rid of some people. Naturally I'd be at the top of the list."

While it was true, it still irritated Mia that Gail had come to that conclusion. "Why would you make that assumption?"

She folded her arms. "Am I wrong?"

Mia couldn't lie to her. She shook her head.

"I'm not done with the budget yet. I'm trying to find options. That's why I haven't mentioned it to you."

Gail leaned forward. "You're a horrible liar, Mia, always have been. You've been avoiding me the last two days, and you've stopped cc'ing me on the budget emails to Chris. I see the writing on the wall, but I'm here to ask you not to do it."

Mia sighed. "I'm sorry, Gail. I will do my best to try and find you something good."

"Oh, I'll find another job in a minute. My old show has been begging me to come back. I'm not worried about me, I'm worried about you."

"Excuse me?"

"Saira. I've been worried about you since you started seeing her."

"That's not fair." Mia and Gail were close but she'd been limited in how much she shared. She didn't need Gail to tell her all that was wrong about her relationship with Saira—her inner critic did a pretty good job of that.

"I've worked with you before. When the show is filming, you are hyperfocused.

On this show, you've been distracted. You haven't been yourself."

"It's the biggest show I've done. There's a lot to do…it has nothing to do with Saira."

Gail pinned her with a hard look. "Tell me something, Mia—are you happy living your life in the closet?"

"What're you talking about?" Mia said wearily.

"You talk about how important it is to live openly, and here you are, sneaking around with a married woman. Tell me, are you enjoying hiding out in hotel rooms? Getting good at looking away when someone catches you staring at her? Having your friends lie for you?"

"Gail… I'm grateful you covered for me and Saira. Our relationship is complicated, I don't deny it. She needs some time to sort things out. She's got a lot of responsibilities. As soon as she finds a good project in LA, she'll come out and our relationship can be more open."

"I hope you're right but are you sure you can trust her? I hear she's signing some big period film for Bollywood."

"What? When did you hear this?"

"There has been chitchat about it for weeks now. Didn't Saira tell you?"

Gail had to be mistaken. There were always rumors and gossip about movie contracts.

"I'm sorry about the budget, Gail…"

Gail stood and gave her a hug. "Take care of yourself. Try and remember why you have your principles."

Mia put her forehead on her desk once Gail left. Her friend's comments had poured salt on the gaping wound that was her relationship with Saira. Hiding, sneaking away was wearing on both of them, but Saira had asked her for time and understanding and Mia had agreed to be patient. But, was Gail right about the effect it was having on Mia's job? Had she been so focused on protecting Saira that she'd jeopardized her show and career? David had accused her of the same thing, of losing control over the star of her show and letting it run over schedule and over budget. She took a breath. If the show got a second season, she would resign as producer. It wasn't fair to the crew if she couldn't handle Saira. She could get another job as producer, but she couldn't replace Saira as the love of her life.

The last month of shooting went smoothly. After Saira's declaration of love, they'd made up, but Mia saw less and less of Saira as their working days got longer and Mia got busier with editing. As much as she hated to admit it, Saira was better at remembering her lines when Mia didn't spend the night at her hotel.

The wrap party to celebrate the end of filming arrived way too soon. Saira was scheduled to leave the next day to see her sister in Geneva. Saira had promised to return to LA in a few days. Though filming had wrapped up, there was always something that came up in the editing process, and sometimes they needed actors to come back in to redub lines in the sound studio.

Mia had a bad feeling about Saira leaving. She couldn't explain what it was, but there was a gnawing ache deep in her belly about saying goodbye to Saira. They were spending the night together, and Saira kept saying it was only a few days that she'd be gone but there was no real reason for Saira to be in LA. She didn't have another project lined up, and Mia was going to be very busy getting the show ready to air.

Mia made it to the hotel before Saira, who had texted to say that she was meeting with Steve and would be late. Mia hoped that Steve had come up with something good for Saira. They'd discussed the offers he'd brought her to date, and Mia hadn't been impressed. As much as she wanted Saira to pick up a project in LA as soon as possible, she knew the offers he'd brought Saira were not right for her.

The smell of flowers greeted her as she opened the hotel room door. A beautiful bouquet of pink and white peonies sat on the dining room table. Mia set down her messenger bag. The envelope with the card was open. Was it wrong to see who the bouquet was from?

Mia picked up the envelope. Saira was a star; plenty of people knew peonies were her favorite. Plus, any number of agents, studio execs, directors, producers, even costars sent flowers to each other, especially on wrap day. But something about the flowers called to her.

She opened the envelope, read the note, then placed it back on the table.

Congrats to the new Mumtaz Mahal. See you in Mumbai soon.

It was from her Bollywood agent. This was the movie David and Gail had told her about. She had asked around about it. There was a big project being financed out of Dubai, a period piece about the wife of the guy who built the Taj Mahal for her. The role was huge, but there was no way Saira would take it. The shooting schedule would be months in India. Saira hadn't even mentioned it to her. They had talked about all the other offers that Saira had received. Mia assumed Saira hadn't brought it up because she wasn't considering it. *She lied to me.* Was she even going to Geneva or was she headed to Mumbai?

Mia sat on the couch and buried her face in her hands. She had written this script from the beginning. Saira was never going to stay. Mia didn't doubt that she wanted to, that Saira loved her. But it took more than love and wanting to do what Saira needed to do, and Mia knew her well enough to know that she wasn't ready. Saira was used to being the heroine—of her family, of her country. She liked taking care of her family, being the provider. She enjoyed being the darling of a country. It was a lot to give up to come live with Mia in a crappy one-bedroom condo.

Saira had asked if Mia would be willing to give up her own life to come be with her. The truth was that Mia didn't have the courage either. Sure, she made excuses: she didn't speak Hindi, or any of the Indian languages; she had no job prospects in India. There wasn't exactly a demand for American TV producers with mediocre titles behind their name. The real issue was that she wasn't ready to go live in hiding, pretending to be Saira's friend or whatever, watching her lover go to parties with her husband and carry on with a fake marriage. This whole time, Mia had assumed she was on the moral high ground, wanting them to live openly. But wasn't she asking Saira for a sacrifice when she wasn't willing to do the same? When Gail had asked her whether she was willing to live in secret, Mia had recoiled. She wanted Saira to give up her whole life and come out, but if Saira seriously asked her to do the same, Mia couldn't.

Saira breezed in late at night. "So sorry I couldn't break away earlier. Steve and I had a lot to talk about, so we went and had dinner and drinks."

"Good meeting?"

Saira nodded. "He's in discussions to get me a small walk-on role in a really cool espionage thriller movie."

Mia let her go on telling her about the project. Her stomach was in knots, her mouth completely dry. "You got flowers."

Saira hadn't noticed. "Oh…who arc thcy from?"

"Your Mumbai agent. Congratulating you on that role you just took."

Saira froze. "Listen, I was going to talk to you about that."

Mia narrowed her eyes. "When were you going to tell me? After you got to Mumbai, when you wouldn't have to face me?"

"After I got back from Geneva. I'm meeting with the film financiers there. The deal isn't final."

"I thought you were going to Geneva to sort out whatever is going on with Kayra."

"I am. Look, I haven't signed the final papers and the movie financiers want to meet with me. I think they're going to offer me more money. The financiers are from Dubai, and since I was going to be in Geneva, my agent got them to meet me there."

Mia didn't trust herself to speak.

As if reading her mind, Saira took Mia's hands in her own. "I am going to Switzerland to see Kayra. That was always the plan. This meeting only happened yesterday. This role, Mia, it's huge. It has international appeal. Even Steve thinks I should take the role because it'll help me land better in LA. I am only considering this project because it helps me ultimately get to LA."

She was looking at Mia so earnestly it cut through her heart. Saira really believed she was doing the right thing. "How long is the project?"

"Nine to ten months. But that doesn't mean

I'll be gone the entire time. I'll come here, and maybe you can visit me."

"Visit you on set? Where you'll introduce me to everyone as what? Your ex-producer? Your friend? Your former lover? Or your secret girlfriend?"

Saira let go of Mia's hands. "I haven't figured it all out yet."

"Why didn't you tell me you were considering this movie?"

Saira looked away and Mia had her answer.

Mia swallowed against her tight throat. "You and I both know what's going to happen. You're going to go back to India and resume your life as a beloved and happily married star. You'll leave me waiting here for years before finally admitting that you can't give up your life there."

Saira was shaking her head as she spoke. "That's not fair Mia. You haven't even given me a chance. I can't topple my whole life in a day. I have to start with my family, prepare for what's coming. It's about their safety too. You know what happened to Kayra. I can't risk something like that happening to them."

Her eyes were wet and Mia's chest burned. Saira would keep getting sucked into her responsibilities. Until she admitted to herself that she couldn't do it all, she would keep sacrificing her happiness, and Mia's.

Mia sank down on the couch and buried her face in her hands, unable to look at Saira. *I'm tired of waiting for you.*

Saira clicked on her phone and turned it toward Mia. She recoiled. "What is that?"

"That's a picture from a news story about a director I worked with in India. He's openly gay. Some guy threw acid in his face because he thinks Jay is responsible for his son being gay. That's a picture of him in the hospital. He's looking at months of plastic surgery and even then he's never going to look right. This happened just a few days ago."

"That's horrible." Mia sat on the couch and grabbed Saira's hand. "I'm so sorry that happened to your friend."

Saira squeezed her hand. "I know there's a certain risk involved in being a public figure. You get threats and stalkers no matter what. But you have to understand that India is where America was fifty years ago with gay rights—most of them still think the way your parents do. They think that when celebrities come out, they are corrupting their children, Westernizing them. Things are changing, but slowly. It was only 2018 when our Supreme court struck down the penal code that made homosexuality illegal. Until then, police threw people in jail and beat them for no other reason than a neighbor or family member's complaint."

"We've had this conversation so many times, Saira. I understand the risks in India are different than they are here. I thought you were ready to leave, to start a life here with me."

Saira sighed. "I am. I just need more time. We've waited ten years, what's a few more? It's just until my career takes off. Then I can move my family, and we can live together openly."

"That was your plan ten years ago."

It was her fault. Mia knew this was where it was headed from the very beginning, but she'd let herself get sucked into a fantasy.

She cupped Saira's face. "I know you love me. I don't doubt it for a second. But you can't have it all. You can't have your fame, your lucrative movie contracts, keep your sister in that expensive facility, take care of your parents and live your life openly with me. You want things to be perfect for everyone, but that's just not possible. You have to decide, Saira. What are you willing to sacrifice for your happiness? For us?"

Tears streamed down Saira's face. Her own eyes were wet. She'd known they were headed toward this. Had avoided it, tried to tell herself there was a way they could work it out. It was too much to ask of Saira. She wasn't ready yet. Maybe she'd get there, but Mia couldn't spend her life waiting, hoping, living in the shadows.

"Can't you wait, just for a little while?"

The plea in Saira's voice shook her resolve. She could wait for Saira, couldn't she? What was a few years for the love of her life? It's not as if she'd had luck finding a life partner in the last ten years. Except she hadn't been looking for a life partner. Now Mia was ready for permanence. If anything, the time spent with Saira talking about the future, a home, children, date nights—it had helped Mia realized she was ready for all that. She wanted to come home to someone each night, have that special person she could take to the insufferable parties; she wanted to plan a future, including children.

"It's not fair to you or to me to put our lives on hold, waiting, hoping that things will change."

Mia pulled Saira into a hug, closing her eyes and breathing in her scent. Saira kissed the corner of her neck, then her check, and her mouth found Mia's. They kissed with all the pent-up passion of the past ten years, and the future they each knew they wouldn't have. They held each other for a long time, their bodies melded together. Mia finally broke free before she lost the last of her crumbling nerve. "At least we get to say goodbye this time."

She picked up her messenger bag and walked out of Saira's hotel room, and her life.

Seventeen

Saira waited in the family lounge of the Clinique Lake Geneva. The glass wall overlooked snowcapped mountains and a landscaped garden that could've inspired a Monet. She sat on a lemon-yellow sofa that was hard on the back but too stylish not to like anyway. Mia would've hated this place. It was pretentiously beautiful and uncomfortably luxurious. Saira had spent the entire plane trip alternatively crying and arguing with herself. Finally after eight hours, she'd realized that she couldn't give Mia what she wanted. Saira couldn't choose between her own happiness and that of her family. She'd thought about begging Mia to give her more time. Mia was right, it wasn't fair to her.

Kayra came breezing in and gave her a warm hug, which Saira returned. Like last time, Kayra looked happy and healthy and Saira instantly relaxed. Whatever Kayra wanted to talk about, it wasn't bad news.

"Saira, I want you to meet someone." It was only then that Saira noticed a tall man, athletic, with sandy brown hair. He was wearing a stylish khaki jacket, jeans and a black T-shirt.

"This is Paul."

Saira stuck out her hand and Paul leaned in and hugged her. "It is so nice to meet you. Kayra talks about you all the time." He had a European accent that Saira couldn't quite place.

"Well, I must admit that she has kept me totally in the dark about you."

Kayra grinned and pulled Saira back down to the couch. Paul pulled up a chair across from them. "I wanted to tell you in person, after you met Paul. We're in love. Paul wants me to marry him."

Saira looked at Paul, who smiled back at

her. He leaned forward. "I'm in love with your sister, and it's important to both of us that you approve."

"This all sounds wonderful, but how about you start from the beginning. How did you two meet? How did you fall in love? I want to hear it all." Paul and Kayra were only too happy to tell her the whole story. Paul was the son of a Swiss banker. He had come to Clinique Lake Geneva six months ago for a one-month stay. He didn't elaborate on why, just that he was stressed and needed to figure some things out. They fell in love. Initially Paul extended his stay but then his father refused to pay for it, so he'd been visiting every weekend.

"How does your family feel about Kayra?" Saira asked carefully. She was happy for her sister but Paul had yet to mention what he did for a living.

"They think she's been good for me. They've been on me to finish my degree and I've been making really good progress since Kayra's been helping me."

Saira smiled at Kayra. Her sister had managed to do her schooling online and even finish an international bachelor's degree. Saira herself hadn't studied further than the Indian equivalent of high school. It was hard enough to get tutoring on set and find time to study to pass her exams; there had been no time for college, especially once she'd had to start paying for Kayra's medical care. Saira had hoped that eventually Kayra would find a job and become independent.

"So what're your plans after you get married?"

Kayra leaned forward. "That's what we want to talk to you about. Paul needs a year to complete his studies but we don't want to wait to get married. I want him to live here with me."

Saira was sure she'd misheard. "Why would he live here? Don't you have a home of your own?"

He nodded. "I live with my parents, but they're not willing to support us until I finish my degree."

Saira shifted in her seat. She didn't want to rain on Kayra's happiness.

"*Di*, please, Paul makes me so happy. It's only a matter of a year, two tops. Plus, if we're living together, you're just paying a little more for him."

"Kayra, you know I'd do anything for you but… I am not sure I can afford to keep *you* here, let alone Paul too. This place is really expensive, and they just raised their rates."

The look on Kayra's face pierced her heart. Saira grabbed her sister's hand. "I can't afford to pay for you to stay here, but we can work something else out. Maybe you can get an apartment. I'll pay for everything until Paul gets on his feet."

"You want me to leave here?" Kayra's eyes got big. "*Di*, I can't. I feel safe here, I can't go somewhere else."

Saira sighed. She'd had this conversation with Kayra many times. "You have to at some point, Kayra. You can't live here forever. It's a hotel, not a home." She looked at Paul with some hope. "You two will want to start a real life together, in your own home."

Paul nodded at first. "Of course, but we just need a few years, to figure it out, you know. This place, it's so peaceful, so healthful, I can focus on my studies."

It didn't escape her notice that they started

with a year, then two years, and now it was a few years. She rubbed her temples. She could barely afford to pay Kayra's way with the new rates at the facility. There was no way she could pay for Paul too. "Kayra, I'm getting on in age, I have maybe a few more years of being able to earn what I do now. I can't keep paying for you here." She looked at Paul. "I want to help you guys, I really do, but you're going to have to ask your parents for support if you want to live here."

Kayra stood. "So what, you're abandoning me? After everything I've been through because of you."

Saira's mouth soured. "Because of me? If I recall correctly, you wanted to do that movie. You were always jealous that I was the star. You begged me to get you a role."

Kayra's eyes blazed. "And you gave me the one role you didn't want."

"I gave you the only role they'd take you for. Do you think I didn't try? You think Ma didn't try? She sent your photo for every role that came my way. She hounded my agent. I didn't deliberately give you that show. It was bad luck you ended up with that show."

"Luck!" Kayra scoffed. "What luck I have, spending half my life in hospitals and treatment facilities while you get to enjoy the luxuries of being a big star."

Maybe it was the view of the snowcapped mountains, or the appearance of a waitress with three tall glasses of lemonade served in cut glass crystal. Everything that Mia and Rahul had been saying came crashing down. "Luxuries? I've had luxuries? I work eighteen hours a day, nonstop. If I'm lucky, I get Sunday off, and in that time, I think about more ways in which I can make enough money to support the family. Here you are living in the lap of luxury, going to the spa every day, taking nature walks, all charged to my account with no consideration as to what it takes to pay for all this."

"I didn't ask to be here, what happened to me…"

"Was not my fault."

"You're saying it was mine?"

Saira shook her head. "It was bad luck, fate, call it what you want. It was my duty as your sister to get you the best medical care possible, which I did. But now you're asking me not only to pay for you to live in this palace, but also support your fiancé?"

"You know I'm still getting therapy."

Saira tapped on her phone and pulled up the latest report from the center. "Your psychiatrist discharged you two years ago. The therapist you see is a wellness specialist. He's not a medical doctor. There is nothing you're getting here that you can't get at home." Then it hit her. She held up a finger and pulled up the invoice her accountant had sent her when he asked to break one of her fixed deposits to pay for the latest bill from the facility. He'd said the bill was much higher than usual. "Has Paul been living here with you? Have you been putting his expenses on my account?"

Kayra lifted her chin. "It's not that much.... and we had no choice.... I couldn't just see him on the weekends..."

"Do you have any idea how much this place costs? Do you know how much I've been stressing about money. How I'm making decisions based solely on how much money I'll earn? I just broke up with the love of my life because...."

"*Di*, I don't want to hear anything. I love Paul and you'll have to find a way to support us."

How had she never noticed how petulant Kayra was? How spoiled her sister had become? Saira had been so focused on protecting her, shielding her, giving her everything she wanted to make up for what she'd had to go through that she'd never noticed how entitled her sister was. Rahul had been telling her for years that Kayra was like an only child who was given everything she ever asked for.

Saira stood. "I am leaving, Kayra. You can finish out the month here, after that I'll let you know what arrangements I've made. I'm not paying for you to stay here anymore."

Kayra stared at her wide-eyed. "Ma is going to want to talk to you."

So Kayra had already discussed this with her parents. Of course she had. How had Saira missed it? Her parents and Kayra were always on the same page. Against her.

"I'm headed to Mumbai now." It was time for her to have a serious talk with her parents.

* * *

She breathed out when she stepped onto the tarmac at Mumbai airport. It was hot, sticky, and the air smelled of salt, fish and jet fuel.

Her regular car and driver were there to pick her up. She was greeted at her apartment complex by a crowd of fans. Someone had posted her arrival at the airport on social media and despite the early morning hour, a crowd had gathered. She told the driver to stop right before the building gates. She lowered her window and grasped the hands that came forward, blowing kisses at the gathered crowd. A little girl was hoisted on shoulders until she made her way to the car and handed Saira a bouquet of flowers.

Saira asked the girl her name, accepted a kiss on her cheek and took a picture with her. These were the moments she loved.

As she entered the building, the security guards lined up to greet her. There was a new person there she didn't know. He'd been hired a few days ago, and when he stepped forward to introduce himself, she thought about Jay and the acid in his face. Like her, he would've felt perfectly safe walking into his own home, wouldn't think twice about a new face. All that would change if she came out. She would have to live in a bubble, unable to interact with her fans, fearful of anyone she didn't know. Her life would be very different.

Her parents were waiting for her when she arrived. Their two-level, five-bedroom condo smelled as it always did, like sandalwood incense from the morning prayers. The living room was marble white floors, glass coffee and accent tables, and comfortable black leather couches. Her parents greeted her with warm hugs. Her favorite cutting chai, a strongly brewed cup with ginger and cardamom, appeared as soon as she sat down on the couch. She took a sip. "I've missed chai. Americans have no idea how to make a good cup of tea."

Her mother smiled. Parvati Sethi had been a beautiful and talented actress. She claimed her career had been derailed by the arrival of Saira first, then Kayra. Saira never knew what her father really did for a living. He had some family money, which he'd lost early in life, then was involved in several failed businesses. For a while he'd managed her mother's career and then Saira's, until she realized that he couldn't resist starting more businesses than he could manage. As soon as she turned eighteen, Rahul had made her hire a proper accountant. It hadn't been easy to take the power away from her father, but she'd had to do it—at the time, the family was close to losing their home. She took a deep breath as she sipped her chai. If eighteen-year-old Saira had the courage to tell her father he couldn't manage her money anymore, then she could do this now.

"You look tired dear, why don't you go rest for a little while." Her father patted her hand.

"Tell me what you want to have for lunch. I'll have the cook make it," Parvati added.

Saira was exhausted. She hadn't slept on the plane from Geneva. Her head hurt and nothing sounded better than some sleep and the cook's rajma chawal. Their cook had been with them since Saira was a child and old Lata *didi*'s red beans and rice were her comfort food.

She looked at her watch and shook her

head. Due to the fog in Mumbai, the plane had had to delay departure from Geneva. She had a meeting with the movie producers in a couple of hours. The meeting with the financiers in Geneva had gone really well. They'd agreed to 13 percent above her usual fee. The casting wasn't even complete, and *Mumtaz*, as the movie had been named, was already creating buzz.

"I wish I had time to rest but I have a meeting in two hours."

"You sound so tired, *jaan.*" Her mother put an arm around her. "Is everything okay?"

Saira smiled and leaned into her mother, taking some comfort in the way she squeezed her tight.

"I have to talk to you about a few things." She took another fortifying sip of the tea, letting the hot liquid strengthen her.

"Is this about Kayra?" her father asked. "Sweetheart, I know how much pressure you're under trying to launch your Hollywood career, but God willing, your show will be great and then you'll be earning in dollars."

Saira pressed her lips. "Dad, don't you

think it's a bit much to have to pay for Kayra's fiancé, who is perfectly healthy, to stay in that really expensive place?"

"Don't think that way. You're supporting your sister. You know how hard it's been for her to be in a relationship. Paul is a nice guy."

"How would you know?"

"He came to the ashram last month to ask us if he could ask Kayra to marry him. So wonderfully old-fashioned."

The extra charges from the ashram.

"And you paid for him to stay at the ashram."

Her mother frowned. "So what, he was our guest."

"Ma, I had to break one of my fixed deposits to pay last month's ashram and clinic bills. Do you understand what that means? The money coming in couldn't cover the expenses, I had to dip into my savings. I'm getting old now, the leading roles are going to stop coming. We'll have to live off our savings, and then what? How long can that last?"

Her mother pulled her arm away, clearly

upset. How could she not understand? Her mother had gone through the very same thing; when she'd tried going back to acting after taking a break, she'd been told she was too old for leading roles.

"Maybe after the next role it's time for you to start thinking about having children. The next generation."

She can't be serious?

"You want me to have children so I can work them the way I've worked all my life?" She must be misunderstanding her mother.

"What's so bad about the life you had?"

Saira stared at her mother. Rahul and Mia's voices were playing in her head. All her life, she'd vilified Rahul's parents and been grateful for her own family, assumed that they were letting her take care of them because they had no other choice.

"My entire childhood was spent on a set. I can't even remember what's real and what was a scene in a movie. I didn't go to school, play with friends or do anything other than work. I wouldn't wish that life on my children."

Her mother looked away. "If you were that unhappy, why didn't you tell us?"

"What choice did I have? We needed the money and you made it very clear that we'd lose our home if it weren't for the money I was bringing in."

Her parents were silent and Saira downed the rest of the tea. "But there's an even bigger reason why Rahul and I will never have children."

She had their attention now. Saira took a deep breath. This is what she'd come to do, and she had put it off long enough. "I don't love him, not in the way a wife should love her husband. In fact, I never have and never will love a man. I've been a lesbian all my life."

She met her parents' gazes, expecting shock and anger, but they just stared passively back at her.

"Is this about that girl in Fiji?"

She nodded."

Her parents looked at each other and her mother sighed. "When you were a teenager, you were only obsessed with the female actresses. Girls your age had posters of Salman

Khan on their walls, but you had Madhuri Dixit. Then there was Fiji. At first, I thought you were just experimenting, but you were so depressed when we brought you back, it was clear what had happened there."

Saira could scarcely believe what she was hearing. Her parents had known all along. After Fiji, they made it seem as though it had been a one-time thing, that she'd lost her way, that she was experimenting. Saira had spent years agonizing over the decision to tell them that Fiji wasn't just her experimenting, cried buckets of tears over the guilt of how she'd treated Mia. It had all been for nothing. Her parents had known!

"If you knew, why did you push me to marry Rahul?"

"Saira, you're a grown woman now. I thought you understood when I explained it to you back then. You can't live your life like that. You heard what happened to Jay? Forget Jay, you've lived through what happened to Kayra, and that was because she misrepresented a religious figure. It would be one thing if you were a nobody. Maybe you could live your life quietly. But people look up to you. The public will blame you for every young girl that tells her parents she's a lesbian, and they'll take their anger out on you."

It was Saira's turn to look away from her mother. She couldn't argue with anything Parvati said. They were the same concerns and fears she had.

"I can't keep living a lie. I want to come out with the truth, go live in America where I can live openly."

Her mother shot her father a look. "Let me talk to my daughter alone."

Narayan didn't argue; he was more than happy to escape to the upstairs terrace.

Her mother turned to her after he'd left. "Saira, do you think I've spent my life in love with your father?"

It wasn't really a question Saira had thought about. Her parents weren't always lovey-dovey but they seemed to get along.

"Your father has been like my best friend. The same way Rahul is yours. Do you think I don't know about him? I've known both of you since you were children. Do you think any Indian mother would allow her *jawan* daughter to be alone in her bedroom for hours with a boy?"

Saira's eyes widened. "Then why did you want us to marry?"

"Because you are good friends, you understand each other and will keep each other happy. Marriage is not about love and romance. Sex and passion fade, especially when your arthritis kicks in—" she gave Saira a small smile. "—but what endures is when you have an understanding with your partner. When you are willing to share in their successes and their failures. That's what a lifelong marriage is. I knew Rahul would take care of you, treat you well, give you comfort. What can you hope to have with a woman? You will be shunned from India. All those fans that give you flowers and balloons when you walk through the door will throw rotten tomatoes and eggs at you. You want to leave your home and go live in America? Then what? You think you'll live happily ever after as a nobody?"

"I can be an actress in LA. The woman from Fiji, Mia, she's the love of my life. I can be with her there."

"What about us? You think that public, those people that are sitting outside our building right now will leave us alone? Kayra hasn't come to Mumbai because just the sight of the crowds stresses her. How do you think she'll handle the media attention?"

Saira looked away. Her mother grabbed her hand, pulling Saira's attention back to her.

"There was a time when I thought that I could have everything in my life. But I've learned that life is all about compromises. No matter what people say, women really can't have it all. We are mothers, daughter, sisters, and because we are stronger than the fathers, sons and brothers in our lives, we are the ones who make the sacrifices, who hold the family together."

Saira's stomach turned. Wasn't that exactly what Mia had said to her? That she had to choose—between her family's happiness and her own.

Parvati grasped her hands. "We need you to hold this family together. You don't want to pay for Paul, fine. You want us to reduce our expenses, fine. Whatever you say. But don't give up your life on the hope that you'll find happiness with that Mia woman. How long have you known her? Is she willing to give up her life for you?"

Saira bit her lip. Her mother squeezed her hands. "What if it doesn't work out with her? You'll have destroyed your life, and all of our lives—for nothing."

Saira closed her eyes, letting the tears flow down her cheeks. She knew what she had to do.

Eighteen

"Earth to Mia!"

Mia looked at David, who was frowning at her. "I've asked you the same question three times and you are off in space."

"I'm sorry, David. Just a lot on my mind right now."

They were in the screening room reviewing the first episode. The network wanted to release it as soon as possible, even before the other episodes were ready, to garner more interest in the show.

"I know what's on your mind. It's that announcement that Saira's going to star in the Mumtaz movie. She's not coming back and giving you your happily ever after, is she?"

Mia sucked in a breath. "No, she is not." David had become a friend in the last few weeks. Turned out that he was a romantic and a fair share of heartbreaks had inspired his empathy.

He put a hand on her shoulder. "It's for the best. Trust me, actresses are a pain in the ass to deal with. They are so full of themselves, always wanting the spotlight."

That's what I used to think too. "I knew she was going to sign that movie. That's why I broke up with her."

"Still hurts to see it in print. I will say I notice a few more wrinkles on her forehead. I predict she won't age well."

Mia smiled and punched David playfully in the arm. "I appreciate what you're trying to do but it's not necessary."

"She's coming to the release party next month."

Mia sucked in a breath. That, she hadn't heard. "I can handle it." It had been two months since she'd last seen Saira. The last message she'd received from her had been a text—*I love you*—a few hours after Mia had left the hotel room, probably before she left for Geneva. That's it. Nothing since then. No "I've reached Mumbai safely." Or "I miss you." Mia hadn't really expected it, but that didn't stop her from wanting it. She had avoided Saira's social media, but her days had been filled with images of Saira. Even now, her face was paused on the big screen, frozen in a half smile, half smirk. Mia closed her eyes. They had another month of editing before she could take a break. Except, how was she going to get Saira out of her heart and soul?

"You need to get out, meet people."

"I've lost count of how many women Gail has swiped right for me."

"Meet anyone?"

"About five someones." They had all been intelligent, beautiful women. The type of women who were ready to settle down and were perfect matches for Mia. She'd had five great dates, and none of them came close to making her heart beat the way Saira's image on screen did.

"You have to move on."

"Easier said than done."

"So you're going to spend the rest of your life pining for her?"

"Pretty much."

"If the show gets a season two, she'll be back here for several months."

"And will be another producer's problem."

David raised his brows.

"It would be too tempting to fall into her bed again. I can't do that to myself and to her. I won't produce another season."

"So I've been nice to you for no reason?"

Mia smiled. "Total loss for you."

"You wouldn't take up with her, even if you're single?"

Mia shook her head. "It's not the way I want to live my life, sneaking around, pretending… I'm trying to respect that Saira isn't in the same place in her life. But I'm not going to torture myself with stolen moments." She turned away from David. It was so much easier to say than to do. She'd spent every night away from Saira longing for her, crying for her, barely holding on to the last vestiges of control she had left to keep from texting or calling her. She pulled out her phone. “Do you mind if we take a break?”

David shrugged. “I could use a coffee.” As he left, she opened up her Facebook account. Her birthday was two days ago. Her mother had sent the usual message wishing her a happy birthday and asking if she was “normal” yet. It was the only communication she ever received from her parents. The same message every year on her birthday. Mia never responded. She hadn’t talked to her parents since she graduated from high school. They hadn’t even come to her graduation, just signed the final school forms before she turned eighteen. She had lectured Saira about courage, but there was one thing she hadn’t gotten the nerve to do, and it was about time she did.

Mom, I am normal. I always have been and always will be. It’s time you accepted it. If you can’t, please don’t contact me again.

A part of her had been waiting for her parents to come around. She’d never said goodbye to them. It was time to do that. She hit Send on the message.

A text message popped up from Jessica,

the woman she had gone out with two nights ago, one of the dating app matches from Gail's online swiping spree. Jessica was a lawyer, had nothing to do with the entertainment industry and was classically beautiful.

Saira's face was still on screen.

She texted Jessica, inviting her to dinner. It was time to move on.

"You're wearing that to the premiere party?"

Saira twirled in front of the mirror. "What's wrong with it?"

Rahul clicked his tongue. "A little risky, isn't it? Too much on the nose?"

"Are you sure you want to come with me?" she asked.

"I wouldn't miss it for the world. Don't worry, my publicity machine is ready."

Saira took a deep breath. "Are we ready to do this?"

Rahul rolled his shoulders. "We will never be ready. But, it's time."

"I will miss your money. This hotel suite is far better than where the network puts me up." The hotel room was indeed splendid. A top floor suite, it had two bedrooms, a spacious living and dining room and closets that fit all the clothes she'd brought, as well as Rahul's.

Rahul laughed. "You know you get a settlement, whether you want it or not. It's in our prenup."

She shook her head. "I'm not taking it." She applied a last coat of lipstick, checked her makeup one last time in the mirror, then turned to him. "I don't want to be one more person who takes from you, Rahul. I'm fine, really I am. I got a great deal on Mumtaz. They're paying me 1 percent above my usual fee."

"I thought they were giving you a lot more."

"They were, but I negotiated alternative terms."

Rahul offered her his arm. "Shall we?"

The party was being held in the rooftop ballroom of their hotel. Networks didn't always throw lavish premiere parties, but this one was doubling as a PR event. Selected press outlets had invitations. When Rahul and Saira stepped out of the elevators, they were directed to walk down the red carpet so the media could snap pictures.

Saira's eyes searched for Mia but she was nowhere to be found. *What if she doesn't come?* She took a breath as they made their way to the gathered media. It didn't matter whether Mia was here or not. Saira wasn't doing this for Mia. She was doing it for herself.

"Saira, love the dress. Can you tell us what you're wearing?"

Saira smiled. She'd had the dress custom designed. It was a strapless gown that fell to the floor with a front middle slit. It was a beautiful silk in rainbow colors.

"I'm wearing this dress to show my pride, and announce that Rahul and I are getting a divorce."

There were murmurs in the crowd, some in surprise, most in confusion.

"Why are you getting a divorce?" someone shouted.

Rahul put an arm around her. "We're getting a divorce because she's found the woman of her dreams, and I've found the man of mine."

There was a momentary pause before the gathered journalists all began hurling questions at once. Rahul and Saira spent thirty minutes explaining it all before an assistant finally moved them off the carpet. They were immediately accosted by actors and crew who wanted their own scoop of the announcement. It took a while before Saira was able to break free of the crowd and find some quiet on an outside terrace. The night was still warm. She took a deep breath, feeling amazingly free.

"Never a dull moment with you." Saira turned to find Mia, looking gorgeous. She was wearing a strappy emerald green dress that wrapped around her in a way that caught Saira's breath. Mia hated dressing up. Had she done it for Saira's benefit? *I hope she did it for me.*

Saira smiled. "I told you to give me some time and I'd figure it out."

Mia was still standing several steps away, looking wary. "What made you do this now?"

Saira wasn't going to wait for Mia to come running into her arms. She stepped toward her. "I finally realized what you and Rahul were telling me all along—my family has been taking advantage of me. All my life, my parents have made decisions based on what was best for them. I decided it's time for me to choose my happiness over theirs."

Mia stood there, maddeningly still. Saira took small steps toward her. She looked like a deer caught in the headlights, ready to flee any second.

"I know you, Saira. You won't be happy abandoning your family."

She was only a few steps away from Mia, close enough to see the tears in her eyes. "You know me so well. I'm still going to take care of them. Just not in the style they've become accustomed to. I'm giving them the money I'm getting from Mumtaz, plus the apartment we own in Mumbai. They can live a comfortable life with that money if they spend it well. If they don't, then they have to figure out a way to earn some of their own. That includes Kayra. She's an educated woman, who is perfectly healthy and capable. I'm done being their ATM. If there are security concerns, I'll have to figure out a way to pay for that, but I have some ideas."

"What about your career? What about that big movie you just signed?"

Saira could hear the fear in Mia's voice. She couldn't believe it was really happening. Saira could barely believe it herself. She and Rahul had spent the last month planning their announcement. Both of them had lost at least five kilos because they were too anxious to eat. Now that it was done, Saira finally felt like a weight had been lifted off her shoulders, a lifetime of weight. It almost felt surreal, like a dream that she might wake up from.

"Mumtaz might be the last film I do, but I made a deal with them that they'd support my announcement. Turns out the main financier has a son who's trans. He's all about bringing social change."

Saira was close enough to see the tears on Mia's cheeks. She reached out, cupped Mia's face and wiped the tears with her thumbs.

"You shouldn't have done this for me," Mia said softly.

"I didn't do it for you. I did it for me. I knew my family had been been taking advantage of me, but I truly believed that they wanted my happiness. That's why theirs mattered so much to me. But when it came to it, what they wanted was for me to sacrifice my needs and wants for theirs. I am done living my life for them, and in hiding. I don't want to be without you."

She touched her forehead to Mia's. "I love you. I've loved you for more than ten years. If you'll have me, I want us to be together. I want a life with you. I want you to marry me."

Mia closed her eyes, and for a second, Saira thought her knees would give out waiting for Mia to answer. Then Mia lifted her chin, found her mouth and kissed her hard. When she finally pulled away, her eyes were shining. "I love you so much. Do you know how hard I tried to get over you? For more than ten years?"

Saira nodded. "I know exactly how hard. That's why I don't want to live another second without you. So will you stop torturing me? Will you or won't you marry me?"

Mia smiled. "Yes Saira Sethi, I will marry you." She wrapped her arms around Saira's waist. "I will marry you, have your babies,

I'll even produce your show if I must. I'll do whatever it takes to make you happy for the rest of my life."

This time when they kissed, it was with the sweetness of their past and the future to come.

* * * * *